Pounamu Pounamu

Witi Ihimaera

EasyRead Large

Copyright Page from the Original Book

The assistance of Creative New Zealand towards the production of this book
is gratefully acknowledged by the Publisher.

TABLE OF CONTENTS

OTHER FICTION BY WITI IHIMAERA   i

FOREWORD   v

INTRODUCTION TO THIS EDITION   xix

A GAME OF CARDS   1

BEGINNING OF THE TOURNAMENT   18

THE MAKUTU ON MRS JONES   40

FIRE ON GREENSTONE   80

THE OTHER SIDE OF THE FENCE   97

THE SEARCH OF THE EMERALD CITY   148

ONE SUMMER MORNING   162

THE CHILD   246

THE WHALE   264

TANGI   284

OTHER FICTION BY WITI IHIMAERA

Short Stories

Pounamu Pounamu (1972)
The New Net Goes Fishing (1976)
Dear Miss Mansfield (1989)
Kingfisher Come Home (1995)
Ihimaera: His Best Stories (2003)
Ask the Posts of the House (2007)

Novels

Tangi (1973)
Whanau (1974)
The Matriarch (1986)
The Whale Rider (1987)
Bulibasha, King of the Gypsies (1995)
Nights in the Gardens of Spain (1995)
The Dream Swimmer (1997)
The Uncle's Story (2000)
Sky Dancer (2001)
Whanau II (2003)
The Rope of Man (2005)
The Trowenna Sea (2009)
The Parihaka Woman (2011)

Children's Books

The Whale Rider – children's edition (2004)
The Amazing Adventures of Razza the Rat (2006)

For Jane

'ONE OF MY GRANDMOTHERS...' WITI
IHIMAERA, AGED THREE, WITH HIS PATERNAL
GRANDMOTHER, TERIA IHIMAERA SMILER,
GISBORNE, 1947.

FOREWORD

By FIONA KIDMAN

Witi Ihimaera's 1972 collection of stories, *Pounamu Pounamu,* changed the face of literature in Aotearoa New Zealand, paving the way for what would later be known as the Maori Renaissance, an unprecedented flowering and recognition of Maori arts and literature in the 1970s. Over the years, Witi has described these early stories as a response to Bill Pearson's essay, 'The Maori and Literature 1938–1965' (in Erik Schwimmer (ed.), *The Maori People in the Nineteen-Sixties: A Symposium,* 1968). In his essay, Pearson had commented on the absence of published fiction by Maori writers, and noted that our literature lacked the perspective of Maori experience. With the publication of *Pounamu Pounamu,* all of this changed. A rural Maori community and the day-to-day lives of its inhabitants form the cornerstone of the stories, and readers were enchanted. The book long ago achieved the status of a platinum bestseller (determined when a book has sold more than 50,000 copies in New Zealand), as have other subsequent books of Witi's. Millions of words must have been written about the author and the publication of *Pounamu Pounamu.* My account is more personal than critical, a record of that time when Witi published his ground-breaking collection, and we had the mutual good fortune to develop a lasting friendship.

Witi and I met in Wellington early in the spring of 1970. At the time, he was working by day as a journalist at the Post Office and writing in the weekends. Our paths had crossed fleetingly more than once, and certainly we had shared space in the periodical *Te Ao Hou* and in the *Listener,* where Witi's first stories appeared. We were both protégés of a splendid old BBC character, Arthur Jones, who was a script editor in the drama department of what was then the New Zealand Broadcasting Service. It was at a scriptwriting seminar organised by the drama department that we got to know each other. Ours was an instant friendship. Witi has frequently reminded me of the way I was dressed that day: white knee-high boots, a miniskirt and a leather cap. It was enough to catch his attention and he teased me mercilessly as a latter-day Mod. Although there are only four years' difference in our ages, he looked to me like a merry teenager and I kept telling him he should be in school. By the end of that day, we had laughed at a great number of things, and at each other. The day didn't stop after the doors shut behind us, and we found ourselves sitting on the edge of the street, still talking. None of this – or the conversation we had about where we came from – seemed in any way forced or artificial. I had grown up in the North, immersed for periods of my schooling in classes that were predominantly Maori. We felt like a couple of country kids who had hit the Big Smoke. I hadn't felt so alive or joyful since I arrived in the city earlier that year.

What else did we talk about that afternoon? Well, we shared dreams of becoming 'real' writers, and we both felt we had many things to write about. Witi loved the movies. He wanted to 'follow the yellow brick road' and indeed, the symbol of the Emerald City from *The Wizard of Oz* had already begun to appear in his stories. When at last we parted company, he said, 'I reckon we're hitched to the same star, you and me.'

And, as his books began to appear – far sooner than mine, as it happened – he wrote above his autograph in each one a variation of the phrase, 'we are still hitched to the same star'. To one, he added the phrase 'for better or worse'. Indeed, we have shared the ups and downs of our vocation, and supported each other as best we could, never further than a letter or phone call away.

Our friendship deepened over the year that followed that first meeting, as we visited back and forth at Witi and his wife Jane's Hungerford Road house, overlooking Wellington's wild south coast, and at our place in Hataitai. Jane was Pakeha, and my husband Ian is of Maori descent. Our experiences of mixed marriage in the 1960s and early 1970s were acknowledged, but I can't remember that we ever dwelt on it. On the professional front, Witi and I were both encouraged by Robin Dudding, editor of Christchurch-based *Landfall,* who was opening up that journal's pages to less established writers than his predecessor, Charles Brasch, had, including the voices of women writers and multicultural writers.

Witi and Jane were hungry for overseas experience before they settled to having children. In the following year, when they were in London, Witi wrote in intense bursts, a habit he has followed throughout his career. By the time he returned, he had written the balance of the *Pounamu Pounamu* stories, a draft of the novel *Tangi* and also the novel *Whanau,* and he had found a New Zealand publisher at Heinemann, headed by its spirited managing director, David Heap. The release of *Pounamu Pounamu* the following year, clad in a pounamu-coloured cover, was met with instant and tumultuous acclaim. Many Maori identified with the characters in the book, and felt that their lives had been portrayed in a rich and authentic manner. Pakeha readers felt that at last they 'knew' about Maori lives; they had been transported to Waituhi, the village near Gisborne where the stories are set, and caught up in what some perceived as a lyric, idyllic environment that served as a metaphor for all rural New Zealand life. The developing sexual awareness that occurs in 'The Makutu on Mrs Jones' and 'The Beginning of the Tournament' could be anyone's awakening. As grandparents, Nani Miro and Nani Tama have universal appeal. The word 'aroha' appears often, and it presented a renewed sense of love's possibilities. The longing for the bygone was a sentiment widely shared, particularly by the elderly – no more so than in reading 'Fire on Greenstone', the story of a house burning down with all the family mementos. And in a quietly told story called 'The Other Side of the Fence', an English immigrant explores his reaction to having Maori neighbours, in a manner that enlightens but does not unduly threaten Pakeha sensibility. It 'showed' the face of prejudice, without apparently judging it. The Englishman is left to judge himself.

But while I agree that those elements of engagement, humour and nostalgia are present in *Pounamu Pounamu,* it seems to me that a great deal else was going on in the stories. Things are never quite as they seem. Although I strongly identified with the stories, as other readers did, I was also aware that not all was at ease in the wider Maori community, and that the idyll was imperfect. If one knew where to look, there were messages embedded in the text that should have warned readers that a troubled inquiry about racial discrimination was under way. It is not until the very end of 'Fire on Greenstone' that we read:

...The old people, the young children, all helped, but it was no good. The homestead was old and the flames were hungry upon it. By the time the fire brigade arrived, it was too late. Afterwards a Pakeha had tried to comfort Nani Tama by saying, Never mind. He hadn't understood when Nani had said to him: 'All my family, all this whanau, were in that house...'

...The homestead wasn't just four walls and rooms. It was the manawa, the heart of the whanau, the heart of the family...

In short, we are informed that Pakeha bystanders can easily brush aside concepts of 'manawa' and 'whanau', but that, in doing so, they place themselves outside Maori experience. And despite its smiling face, 'The Other Side of the Fence' delivers a sharp message when the English wife in the story reflects on how misunderstood she is for criticising the Heremaia children next door:

...she at least tried to keep the bad behaviour of the Heremaia children in context. They were not always bad.

As the reading public absorbed the stories, there was much that was going on in the Ihimaera lives, and in literary life in general. The ground was shifting, in a way that at first was almost indiscernible. Robin Dudding left *Landfall* and moved to Auckland, visiting us en route. Witi was among the several writers who came over to Hataitai and talked far into the night, discussing Robin's plans for a new periodical,

Islands, which would free him of the constraints he had felt at Caxton Press to publish and be damned, as it were.

Meanwhile, New Zealand's best-known book lover, the Labour Prime Minister Norman Kirk, read *Pounamu Pounamu* and invited Witi to join Foreign Affairs as a diplomat, a post he accepted. Witi and Jane moved house to Roy Street on the fringe of Newtown, a street with old-world, well-kept charm, enhanced by rows of magnolia trees forming an avenue, glorious in spring. We picked out the Ihimaera house easily, next door to an imposing bust of Bertrand Russell, as we approached.

But if the Roy Street house looked outwardly peaceful, the conversation inside was decidedly colourful. Now, when we visited, we found Maori intellectuals and teachers in heated discussion, formulating ways for change. I found myself being challenged on more than one occasion, and doubts had begun to creep in to my own belief that I could write from a Maori perspective. The mood was charged, radical and often decidedly subversive.

That year, too, *Pounamu Pounamu* was placed third at the 1973 Wattie Book of the Year Award. What happened there carried a potent message. The sponsor was Sir James Wattie, famous for his canned-food processing plant in the Gisborne area, where Witi's family lived, and a well-known horse breeder as well. When Witi stepped forward to receive his prize, Sir James shook his hand, and said: 'Oh, a lot of your people work for me, Mr ... uh, uh,' and here he stumbled helplessly.

'Ihimaera,' Witi said, the smile never leaving his face. 'It has the same number of syllables as your racehorse, Even Stevens.'

The following month, Robin published a new story of Witi's in *Islands,* called 'Clenched Fist'. A friend comes to visit the narrator in his office. Some tourists had just taken the friend's photo out of a bus window.

He was sitting on George's desk at work. Afro hair and air of brooding ruthlessness. Leather jacket scrawled with a peace sign. Dark glasses. Round his neck, Mexican beads.

–I could have mangled the white bastard. I tell you, brother, we're just objects, caged animals in a zoo, entertainment for the tourists. Bloody Yanks, yeah.

He fumbled at George's smokes, lit one and puffed angrily.

Later, as the story progresses, he accuses the narrator of being 'Middle class Maori. Suit. Tie. Aura of conservatism. Antiseptic. Sold out to the pakeha. Uncle Tom.' They continue on, the narrator reminding his friend that, like him, he has Pakeha blood in his veins. An uneasy truce descends, although the quarrel is unresolved. The narrator walks out into the street, where a woman is nearly knocked down by a speeding car. The occupants shout, 'Get back. Get back you black bitch.' The bystanders are amused, except for the narrator, who stands trembling with rage. Without thinking, he raises a clenched fist to the sun.

I was one of the judges the following year when *Tangi,* written in London three years earlier, won the Wattie Book Awards. It was a day to remember. Because of fog, the

Wellington – Christchurch flight was delayed. Witi, Jane and I, along with the other two award winners, set off in a light plane to Blenheim, and from there by car to Christchurch. We didn't make it in time for the awards ceremony. Witi and Jane were preoccupied with the news that they were expecting their first child. I remember that, while Witi was overjoyed by this development, he was at times a little withdrawn. When he learned that he had won first prize, a look of shock passed over his face. I wondered, for a moment, if it was something he didn't really want.

A year or two later he wrote to me from Canberra, where he had taken up a diplomatic posting, and told me that what he loved about being in another country was the feeling of anonymity; that being so well known in New Zealand had become hard. I still didn't see it coming, but I should have. The yellow brick road had got rocky. Although there were still two more books to appear, a time of silence was about to descend. The last book stemming from that period was *The

New Net Goes Fishing, another collection of short stories that included 'Clenched Fist'. For ten years Witi would place himself in publishing exile, for the most part observing his country in private, and from afar. From 1977 until the publication of *The Matriarch* in 1986, Witi published no more books. When he emerged, it was from a position of strength and commitment to the season of change that had been envisaged in the house in Newtown. What I had witnessed, through these unfolding events, was a man defining himself not just as a 'Maori writer' but maturing as a radical thinker and reformer.

He and I have often joined forces. We were at each other's side the night when, with a wider group of writers, we stopped the proceedings in Parliament during the 1981 Springbok tour. We did this by the simple expedient of entering the public gallery, donning black armbands, and reciting the Speaker's prayer as the evening sitting began, thereby breaking the rules of Parliament which require that the Speaker's prayer be heard in silence. After the police had evicted the group, we were collectively banned from Parliament for a year.

This act of solidarity seemed like a seal on our friendship, one that remains steadfast to this day, despite many changes in our circumstances. Forty years on, there is no doubt in my mind that *Pounamu Pounamu* is among the most important books published in this country. Its influence on bicultural understanding cannot be underestimated. That it remains consistently in print after so many years is a testimony to the way we as a people began to re-evaluate, and ultimately reinvent ourselves. It has been through many appraisals and reappraisals by critics and by the writer himself. Ultimately, it is both the healing touch and the fire that burns.

Fiona Kidman

INTRODUCTION TO THIS EDITION

E kore au e ngaro
He kakano i ruiruia mai
i Rangiatea

E nga rangatira ma, tena koutou katoa.

Pounamu Pounamu was published in 1972 and was my first book. The stories in it are about growing up Maori during 'the greenstone years' of my childhood: those years when the rural village and the marae were the centre of our universe. I called the book after the treasured jade which is symbolic of those things in life that are to be prized above all others.

I honour the stories of *Pounamu Pounamu* and, when I hold the jade up to the light, it is just as strong, translucent and beautiful as ever. Ten years ago, in 2002, however, I saw that the light refracted just a little differently and I was able to see more of the roimata toroa, the tears, that are in the jade. They are the dark markings that have always resided there but how you see them and what you see in them all depends on your point of view. Thus, although the stories in this edition of *Pounamu Pounamu* are the same as in the original edition published, they are also different. I have added what I have seen as the light has glanced off, reflected through and highlighted other roimata in the depths of the greenstone. I've rewritten the stories, to show that not only is pounamu a living stone but stories also live, change and are enriched by the dynamic of changing times.

I've also been thrilled to take the opportunity, in this Anniversary publication, to provide a historical and personal context to the book. I've gone back in my memory to the times when I began writing, the 1970s, and provided notes on how the stories all originated. More importantly, I've returned in my memory to Waituhi, all my whanau, to show how both they and Waituhi illuminated my life. They gave me a place and a people to write about; without them there would have been no *Pounamu Pounamu* or, even, a writing career. The notes follow the stories. I hope you enjoy them.

The stories in *Pounamu Pounamu* are about resilience, survival, facing and surmounting challenges and carrying on. My father liked to say to me, during the many times I was ready to give up, 'You are a seed planted at Raiatea! Your ancestors didn't paddle their canoes all that way across the ocean and settle in Aotearoa just to see you strand them in the second millennium! Strike out for the horizon! Paddle on! Their journey won't be over until we reach the stars!'

This edition of *Pounamu Pounamu* is dedicated to that unending quest for the fulfilment of dreams that began long before any of us were born.

You are from a seed that was sown in Rangiatea and you will never be lost

Witi Ihimaera

A GAME OF CARDS

The train pulled into the station. For a moment there was confusion: a voice blaring over the loudspeaker system, people getting off the train, the bustling and shoving of the crowd on the platform.

Then, there was Dad, waiting for me. We hugged each other; we hadn't seen each other for a long time. But I could tell something was wrong.

'Your Nani Miro,' he said. 'She's very sick.'

Among all my kuia, Nani Miro was the one I loved most. It wasn't one way either: everybody used to say I was her favourite mokopuna, and that she loved me more than her own children who'd grown up and had kids of their own. She lived down the road from us next to Rongopai meeting house in the old homestead which everybody in Waituhi called 'Miro's Museum' because it housed the prized possessions of the whanau—the feather cloaks, greenstone ornaments, and the shields and trophies which Waituhi had won in sports and culture tournaments. As children we always used to think she was rich because she owned the most shares in what remained of our tribal land. We wondered why she didn't buy a newer, more modern house. But Nani wasn't thinking of moving.

'Anyway,' she used to say, 'what with all my haddit kids and their haddit kids and all this haddit whanau being broke all the time and asking me for money, what have I got left to buy a new house with?'

The truth was, that Nani liked her old homestead just as it was and didn't really care about money either.

'Who needs it?' she used to ask. 'What you think I had all my kids for, eh? What you think I have all my mokopuna for! To look after me, I'm not dumb!'

Then she would laugh to herself. But it wasn't true, really, because her family would send their kids to her place when they were broke and she looked after them! She liked her mokopuna, but not for too long. She'd ring up their parents and say:

'When you coming to pick up your hoha kids! They're wrecking the place!'

I used to like going to Nani's place with the rest of my cousins. In particular, I looked forward to Saturdays because that's when all the women would take the day off, and turn up to play cards. Nani loved all card games—five hundred, poker, canasta, pontoon, whist, hearts, euchre—you name it, she could play it.

The sitting room would be crowded with the women. There they'd be, dressed in their best clothes, sitting at various tables among the sports trophies and photographs, the carvings and greenstone. In those days, Maori used to be heavy smokers, so the women would all be puffing clouds of smoke, laughing and joking and gossiping about who was pregnant—and relishing all the juicy bits too.

Nani Miro was always at what was called 'the top table', reserved for the best players. Both she and Mrs Heta were the unrivalled champions and when it came to cards Mrs Heta, whose first name was Maka, was both Nani's best friend and worst enemy.

'You ready to be taken down?' Mrs Heta would ask. 'Oh, the cards are really talking to me today.'

'Is that so, Maka?' Nani would answer. 'We'll have to see about that, won't we?'

The women would begin to play cards. No doubt about it: Nani Miro and Mrs Heta were the queens of the game. They also happened, whenever they didn't have the right cards, to be the biggest cheats I ever saw.

Mrs Heta would cough and reach for a hanky while slyly slipping a card she wanted from beneath her dress. You never saw anybody reneging as much as she did in five hundred—and expecting to get away with it! But her greatest asset was her eyes which were big and googly. One eye would look straight ahead while the other swivelled around, having a look at the cards in the hands of the women sitting next to her.

'Eeee! You cheat,' Nani would say. 'You just keep your eyes to yourself, Maka tiko bum.'

Mrs Heta would look at Nani, highly offended. Then she would sniff and say,

'You the cheat yourself, Miro Mananui. I saw you sneaking that ace from the bottom of the pack.'

'How come you know I got an ace, Maka?' Nani would say. 'I know you! You dealt this hand, and you stuck that ace down there for yourself, you cheat! Well, ana! I got it now! So take that!' She would slap down her hand. 'Sweet, eh?' she would laugh. 'Good? Kapai?' Sometimes she would do a little hula, making her victory sweeter.

'Eeee, Miro!' Mrs Heta would reply. 'Well, I got a good hand too!'

And she would slap her hand down and bellow with laughter.

'Take that!'

And always they would squabble. I often wondered how they ever remained friends. The names they called each other!

Sometimes, I would go and see Nani Miro when she was by herself, playing patience. That was her game whenever there was nobody around to play with her. And still she cheated! I'd watch her hands fumbling across the cards. I'd hear her say, 'Oops,' as she turned up a jack or queen she needed, and I'd join her laugh of triumph: 'See, mokopuna? I'm too good for this game!'

Nani used to try to teach me some of the games, but I wasn't very interested.

'How are you going to do good things for your people if you can't concentrate?' she would ask. 'Here I am, counting on you to get a good education so that you can get the rest of our land back and you're just hopeless, he hoha koe—'

Not only that, but I didn't yell and shout at her like the women did. She liked the bickering.

'Aue,' she would sigh. Then she'd look at me, offer words of wisdom that didn't make sense like, 'Don't let me down,' or 'If you can't beat the Pakeha one way remember that all's fair in love—or cards,' and deal out the cards in the only game I ever knew how to play.

'Snap!' I would yell as she let me win.

Now, my kuia was sick.

I went to see Nani Miro that afternoon after I'd dropped my suitcase at home. The koroua, Nani Tama, her long-suffering husband, opened the door. We embraced and he began to weep on my shoulder.

'You talk to her, moko,' he said. 'She walked out of the hospital yesterday. She should go back there. It's no use me trying to persuade her; she's still as stubborn as, never listened to anything I say. But you—'

'I'll do my best,' I answered.

I walked down the hallway, past the sitting room to Nani Miro's bedroom. The room had a strange antiseptic smell. The window was open. Sunlight shone brightly on the big bed in the middle of the room. Underneath the bed was a big chamber pot, yellow with urine.

Nani Miro was lying in bed. Her pillow was flecked with small spots of blood where she had been coughing. She was so old looking. Her eyes were closed, her face was very grey, and her body was so thin, seeming to be all bones. Even when I was a child she must have been old, but I had never realised it. She must be over seventy now. In that big bed, she looked like a tiny wrinkled doll.

Then I noticed the lipstick. Hmmn.

'You can wake up now, Nani,' I said sarcastically.

She moaned. A long, hoarse sigh grew on her lips. Her eyelids fluttered, and she looked at me with blank eyes ... and then tears began to roll down her cheeks.

She took me by surprise. 'Don't cry, kui,' I said. 'I'm sorry. I'm here.'

But she wouldn't stop. I sat beside her on the bed and she lifted her hands to me. 'Haere mai, mokopuna. Haere mai. Mmm. Mmm.'

I bent within her arms and we pressed noses. Then she started to shake with mirth and slapped me hard.

'Snap!' she said.

She started to laugh and laugh and I was almost persuaded she was her own self. But I knew she wasn't. Why do people you love grow old so suddenly?

'What a haddit mokopuna you are,' she grumbled, sitting up in the bed. 'It's only when I'm just about in my grave that you come to see me.'

'I couldn't see you last time I was home,' I explained. 'I was too busy.'

'There's no such thing as being too busy to see your kuia,' Nani reproved. 'Next time, make time. If you don't I'll cut you out of my will. I'll give it all to Willie Jones, what do you think of that?'

'Go right ahead,' I answered. 'Willie will need every cent to pay his fines so he doesn't go to jail.'

Willie was my cousin. When I was growing up I always thought that I was the only one Nani Miro talked to about getting an education. Ha, it was Willie who told me she talked to everybody, but I was the only one to take her seriously. Nani liked to spread her bets. That way, one of her cards was bound to do the trick.

'Anyhow,' I continued, 'I heard Maka cleaned you out in your last game of poker!'

'Who told you that?' Nani scoffed. 'You know, now that she's old she's gone colour blind. Can't tell a heart from a spade.'

She gave a big, triumphant grin. She was my Nani again. The Nani I knew.

We talked for a long time. She wanted to know how I was getting on at university in Wellington. I told her I was doing really well with my studies, which was a lie, because I was seriously brainless and all the ambitions she held for me were rapidly going down the drain. She asked if I had a girlfriend so I made up more lies about who I was seeing and how pretty she was.

'You teka,' she said. 'Who'd want to have you!'

I brought up the subject of her returning to hospital.

'Tama's been talking to you,' she grumbled. 'Well, this is why I came home—'

She showed me all her injection needles and pills.

'I didn't like all those strange nurses looking at my bum when they gave me those injections. I was so sick, mokopuna, I couldn't even go to the lav. Better for Tama to give me my injections. Better for me to wet my own bed and not their hospital bed.'

I played the piano for Nani. She loved *Me he manu rere* so I played it for her and we had a sing-along. Afterwards, she held my hands tightly in hers as if she didn't want to let me go, and stared deep into my eyes.

'It's always the women who look after the land,' she said, 'but who will do it after I am gone?'

When I finally left her I told her I would come back in the morning.

But that night the koroua, Nani Tama, rang up. Dad answered the telephone and woke me.

'Your whaea, Nani Miro, she's dying.'

We all rushed to Nani Miro's house. It was already crowded with the other Waituhi families: the Tamateas, Tuparas, Waitaikis, everybody. All of Nani Miro's mates were crowded close around her bed. Among them was Nani's rival, Mrs Heta. Nani was lying very still. Then she looked up, saw Mrs Heta and whispered to her:

'Maka ... Maka tiko bum ... I want a game of cards.'

A pack of cards was found. Everyone sprang into action. The old ladies sat on the bed, began to gossip and, as usual, puff their clouds of smoke. Nani Tama suggested a game of poker in the living room, so all the men trooped in there to do some serious gambling.

Wherever there was a table—in the kitchen, on the verandah, anywhere, games of cards started up. The kids played snap in the other bedrooms and, as the night progressed, so did the games, the laughter, the aroha. The house overflowed with card players, even onto the lawn outside Nani's window.

Suddenly, there was a commotion from Nani's bedroom. We all looked to see what was happening. The women had been betting on who would win the best of ten games and Nani and Mrs Heta were neck and neck—and Mrs Heta was squabbling with Nani because it was Nani's turn to deal.

'Eee, Miro,' Mrs Heta said, 'don't think that just because you can deal fast I'm not on to your tricks.'

'Quit moaning and start playing,' Nani answered. 'Well?'

'Dealing all the good cards to yourself,' Mrs Heta muttered. 'You cheat, Miro.' And she made her googly eye reach far over to see Nani's cards.

'You think you can see, Maka tiko bum?' Nani coughed. 'You think you're going to win this hand, eh? Well, eat your heart out and take that!'

She slammed down a full house.

The other women goggled at the cards. Mrs Heta looked at her own cards. She did a swift calculation and yelled:

'Eee! You cheat, Miro! I got two aces in my hand already! Only four in the pack. How come you got three aces in your hand?'

Everybody laughed. Nani and Mrs Heta started squabbling as they always did, pointing at each other and saying:

'You the cheat, not me!'

And Nani Miro said:

'I saw you, Maka tiko bum, I saw you sneaking that card from under the blanket.'

She began to laugh. Her eyes streamed with tears.

While she was laughing, she died.

Everybody was silent. Then Mrs Heta took the cards from Nani's hands and kissed her.

'You the cheat,' she whispered. 'Yes, Miro, you the cheat yourself—'

Ma wai ra e taurima
E te marae i waho nei?

We buried Nani Miro on the hill with the rest of her family. During her tangi, Mrs Heta played patience with Nani, spreading the cards across the casket.

Later in the year, Mrs Heta, she died too. She was buried right next to Nani so that they could keep on playing cards.

I bet you they're still squabbling up there.

'Eee! You cheat, Miro!'

'You the cheat, Maka tiko bum. You, you the cheat.'

Whaia te iti kahurangi,
Me te tuohu, he tuohu
Ki te maunga teitei

A GAME OF CARDS

When I was a young boy, I was raised by many grandmothers.

One of them was my beloved Nani, Mini Tupara, who lived at Waituhi, not far from Gisborne. She was my father's auntie but he called her sister because he had been brought up with her. She lived in what people called 'The Blue House' because it was painted that colour; the house is still there, the first house on the lane opposite Takitimu Hall on Lavenham Road.

My father, Tom, was Waituhi born and bred. He was a shearer and scrubcutter and when he and Mum had work, my sister Caroline and I were looked after by various friends and relatives including Nani Mini and her handsome husband George Tupara. It was Nani Mini who sent me off to school at Patutahi and was waiting for me on my return home. When she asked me what I had learnt I recited 'Jack and Jill'. Her reply was 'Who are Jack and Jill? What are they doing going up a hill to fetch water, what a stupid place to put a well!' The next day on my return home, I wasn't so keen to tell her that what I had learnt that day was a poem about Little Miss Muffet. She asked, 'What's a tuffet? What are curds and whey? And why is the little girl so afraid of a spider! She should have picked it up and said kia ora to it.' Nani Mini taught me to ask questions and to be always aware that I was going out into a world where people put wells on tops of hills and where things would not necessarily make any sense.

When I was seven, Mum and Dad moved Caroline and me – and we had been joined by two more sisters, Polly and Vicki – to the house Dad was finally able to buy from his shearing income at 11 Haig Street, Gisborne. So there I was, with one foot in one culture and the other foot in another, but still with huge love for Waituhi. Indeed, whenever we visited Waituhi, Nani Mini was the person I would always look for first. 'Where's Nani Mini?' I would ask, until I found her. In appearance she had the look of a Peruvian Indian, short, compact, strong, eyes burnt black by the sun. She gave me a lot of hugs, but woe betide if I was disobedient, because Nani also had a tongue on her. She had a piano in the house and because I was learning music, she liked me to play it for her; my cousin, called Little Mini to separate her from Big Mini, has told me that I was the only one of the mokopuna allowed to play it. Some of the keys weren't working though and, even today, when I listen to 'Me He Manurere' or other songs of those times, my ear wants to hear 'Me'e manu'e'e' with spaces in it where the keys didn't sound.

Later I left Gisborne, but on one visit home from Wellington as a young man, Dad met me at the railway station and told me that Nani Mini was very sick.

I like to think of this story as being my Queen of Hearts story. Ever since it was published, it's been my calling card.

BEGINNING OF THE TOURNAMENT

The phone rang just as I got back to the flat. It was Dad, ringing from Waituhi.

'Hello, son,' Dad said. 'Are you coming home for Easter?'

'I'm not sure,' I answered but, even as I said the words, I could sense Dad's disappointment. 'It's just that I'm broke at the moment,' I continued, floundering for a reason. 'If you give me a loan, I'll give you the time.'

'A loan?' Dad laughed. 'I'd rather put the money on a horse; at least that way I'll have a chance of getting my money back.'

'So what's on in Waituhi?'

'The Maori hockey tournament,' Dad explained, offended. 'Surely you haven't forgotten that it's Waituhi's turn to host. I want you to come home and to help out. Not only that, but the Waituhi men's team is short.'

'Okay,' I answered.

'Can you bring a mate?' Dad asked. 'When I say our team is short, I mean it's really short.'

'Don't you worry, Dad. I'll see what I can do.'

Later that day I asked Jerry Simmons if he'd like to come home with me at Easter. Jerry was a Pakeha mate of mine who was a good hockey player. Actually, we were university students and had made plans to go with the university ski club at Easter to Mount Ruapehu. Jerry had visions of pulling a few women.

'Every year the East Coast has a hockey tournament with a dance afterwards,' I told him. 'The teams come from all over the Bay.'

I could tell Jerry was disappointed at this change in plan. 'I didn't know you blokes had separate tournaments,' he said.

'For tennis, rugby and golf too,' I answered. 'As far as my family is concerned, though, the hockey tournament is the most important. The supreme trophy in the men's competition is for my grandmother's shield.'

'How big a tournament is it?'

'Well...,' I began, uncomfortably, 'once upon a time the tournament used to attract over fifty teams, but big Maori events have been declining in our area for some time. As more and more people leave for the cities there's less and less people at home. We don't always go back. We're probably down to around twenty-five teams that still arrive for the hockey though. I guess that makes the tournament more important than it ever was. Anyway, you'll see when you get there.'

'I haven't said I'm coming yet! Don't rush me, don't rush me.'

'I've got a terrific looking sister,' I said, giving Jerry a wink. That did the trick. I had told Jerry a lot about Mere and how pretty she was. Anyone would know by just looking at me, that any sister of mine would be pretty: I'm quite a handsome fella myself. But I hoped Jerry wouldn't be too wild with me when he met Mere.

Easter came and, although Jerry moaned about not going to Mount Ruapehu, we started off in the car for Waituhi. It was a long journey and, as

I'd been out rather late the night before, I wasn't in the best of moods when Jerry began pestering me about Mere.

'Is she really pretty? Is she really pretty?' he kept asking.

I got so sick of it I couldn't resist teasing him. 'She's terrific,' I answered. 'She's tall for her age, but not as tall as you. Good figure, long legs, eyes that smile right at you, and a mouth that's just waiting to be kissed.'

As I was describing Mere, however, I began to realise, hey, Jerry was a bit of an animal. No way would I ever want any woman I knew, no matter what age she was, to even be in the same room with him.

'She hasn't got a boyfriend already, has she?'

'Come to think of it,' I answered, backing off, 'I think there might be somebody who's got his eye on her.'

Did Jerry get the joke? Nah. When he met Mere he gave me a dirty look. She was seven, and Jerry saw her playing with her dolls when Dad opened the door.

'So you came,' Dad said, as if he hadn't been too sure I would. 'I thought you might have been studying too hard or having too good a time down there in Wellington.' My father was like the sky above me, wide open, embracing, filling my life with sunlight. There's so much love between us, and I regretted the earlier hesitation about coming. Yes, Dad, I was studying hard and having a good time. But you called and I came.

I forgot all about Jerry until he pounced on me after dinner. 'I should have known better than to trust you! Good figure, huh! Long legs, long hair, a mouth just waiting to be kissed!'

'Easy on! Take it easy, Jerry! I was only joking. Wait. Where will violence get you? Wait! Listen, Jerry! I've got this fantastic looking cousin and...'

But Jerry wasn't going to be taken twice. He was really sorry though when he discovered that this time I was actually telling the truth.

The next morning I woke at dawn and went up to the family graveyard to pay my respects to my kuia, Nani Miro. She had died at the end of winter. Somebody had stuck an Ace of Hearts onto her grave, and small windmills whirred brightly with the wind. Then I saw Dad waving from the homestead and went to join him.

'Miro would have been pleased that you came home to help out,' Dad said. 'I've had to take on a lot of the responsibilities she had for Waituhi. And somebody—' he nudged me hard, to make sure I took the hint—'will have to take it on when I go. Never forget your obligations to your family and to your iwi.'

We had breakfast, I helped Dad sort out the programme for the day and, because Jerry was still sleeping, we left him to get breakfast started for the visitors at Takitimu Hall. Dad stayed there while I went to finish marking up the grounds where the hockey games would be played. By the time Jerry arrived, quite a few of the bystanders had joined me and some of the teams were practising. Jerry had polished his boots and put on his socks and shorts. When he saw the hockey grounds he was horrified.

'Is this it?'

'Yes, Jerry.'

'You mean this ... this paddock?'

'Yes, Jerry.'

An hour later, Jerry was still wandering around, dazed. I'd begun introducing him to the multitude of my relatives and there was not a white one in sight. The buses had started to arrive from Takitimu Hall and the tournament was gradually gaining some semblance of order. A tent had been put up in the paddock, and my Auntie Annie was doing great business selling soft drinks and lollies to the local kids.

'You should have warned me,' Jerry said. He cast a gloomy eye over the crowd. They all seemed to be wearing gumboots or old dresses, balaclava hats, holey jerseys and baggy pants. He knew he looked oh so clean.

Indeed, as one of the men's teams walked past one of them said, 'Ace, man, somebody's brought me a Pakeha to make really dirty.'

'Don't take any notice of them,' I said to Jerry as he went even whiter. 'Anyway, you'll be a sure hit with the girls.'

'I can just see it,' he said sarcastically, glancing at the group of little kids who were following him, pointing at him and giggling. But before he could brood any more, the tournament began.

Nani Kepa wandered onto the field, shooed away a couple of cows, and shouted into a megaphone. 'People, would you please remember to close the gate when you come onto the paddock?' he asked. 'Otherwise you're all going to put your feet into some rather embarrassing substances.' He announced that it was time for the Grand Parade.

'What's that?' Jerry asked.

'Before the games begin,' I told him, 'all the teams parade around the field and the best-dressed team wins a cup.'

'You've got to be joking.'

'No,' I answered. 'Come on!'

I pulled Jerry over to where the Waituhi men's team was standing. All four of them: Dad, Uncle Hepa, Boy Boy and Hone. Now we were six. We needed five more.

'Mo-Crack will be here any minute,' Dad said. 'He's coming from the pub. Then Frank'll be here after he's dropped

Bub at her work. That makes eight, enough for the parade. Come on, boys.'

We followed Dad onto the field where all the other teams were milling: eight other men's teams and sixteen women's teams from the Coast. The women, naturally, were dressed in uniform. One of the men's teams was too. But the rest ... well...

'I feel so conspicuous,' Jerry muttered as we were marching around the field. I couldn't help but agree. Apart from being a head taller than anybody else, Jerry was also the only one with red hair and freckles. Not only that but he was spotless as.

'Hey, Pakeha,' somebody laughed. 'See that cowpat? It's got your name on it.'

Dad consoled Jerry. 'We'll protect you,' he said. Dad turned to me. 'That was a great idea for you to bring such a well dressed friend with you. With him on our side we're bound to win the parade.'

We all laughed and, by the time the parade had lined up to be judged, Jerry was feeling more at ease.

Nani Kepa and a woman from an East Coast team were the judges. They wandered along the ranks of the women's teams, inspecting the dressage, uniforms and overall appearance as if the women were on military parade. Nani Kepa's eagle eyes darted here and there, making sure that socks had been pulled up to the right length, shirts were tucked in and boots polished and laced properly. Competition for the parade was always a more serious business for the women than the men—and, after all, there was more at stake than just a hockey match. You think these girls had taken hours to glam themselves up just for a walk around a cow paddock? Get real. They were here to find boyfriends too or, at the very least, a date for the dance—and get that cup and their brief shining moment of stardom.

Nani Kepa and the woman from the East Coast team went into a huddle. They announced the winner. Unfortunately, that winner happened to be the team of which the woman judge was captain. There was great applause from their followers and catcalls from their rivals. 'Favouritism! Favouritism!'

'I must say that that's a bit unfair,' Jerry said.

'Actually,' I explained, 'it's a good decision. That team hasn't won for a few years and it's their time this year.'

The judges took less time over the men's teams. The woman judge took a shuddering look at the motley lot and hastened quickly over to the only men's team which was wearing uniforms. However, on the way the clouds opened and the sun blazed down on Jerry in all his flawless glory. That did it. The woman judge came staggering over to our team to make sure that she wasn't having a vision and then pointed a finger at him.

'Oh yes,' she said, taking a closer look. 'You are most definitely the winner.'

The crowd clapped and cheered. The few derisive hoots were soon booed out of existence.

'But that other team should have won!' Jerry said.

'They always win,' I answered. 'It's about time they lost.'

'No, it's not that,' Dad said, winking at Jerry. 'Didn't you see the way that lady judge was looking at you, boy? You better watch out. She's a man-eater!'

Then Nani Kepa rang the cowbell again, which meant that the games were to start. He announced the first round: a game between two of the women's teams. The fun began. The women began yelling to one another.

'We got enough sticks?'

'Who's worrying about sticks! Worry about whether we got enough players first!'

'Hey, Huria! Put the baby down and come and be our left wing, eh?'

'Which side is left!'

'What about Nani Marama? What about asking her to play for us? She used to be a good player.'

'Yeah, fifty years ago maybe, when she was twenty.'

'Well, she can still stand on her legs and walking stick, can't she? She can be our goalie. So how do you play this game again? I've forgotten.'

'So have I! Hey, Cissie, what's the rules!'

'Don't you girls worry. Look, you hold the stick this way and you try to hit the ball over into the other side's goal. Not that one, that's ours. The other one. See? It's only easy.'

All this time Jerry was just standing there, stunned.

'I don't believe it,' he said, as he saw the women taking the field. About half were dressed in uniforms, so one could assume they knew what they were doing. As for the others, well, Huria was hitching her skirt into her pants, Nani Marama was borrowing Nani Kepa's glasses so she could see where the goal was, and Cissie was still yelling to other girls to come and help out. Among them was my cousin Moana, who was actually supposed to be playing for another team.

'Be a cuz, Moana!'

'But I've left my stick in the bus!' Moana answered.

Jerry came to the rescue. 'You can borrow mine,' he said.

Moana was the fantastic looking cousin I had actually tried to tell Jerry about. Not that I needed to. I saw the way she and Jerry looked at each other and, even though it was a sunny day, I had the uneasy feeling that both had been struck by lightning. It was one thing to introduce Jerry but did I actually want it to go any further?

'What a babe,' Jerry said.

No, no, three times no. 'Don't even think about it,' I warned him.

The game began. It was a match showing all the expertise of military manoeuvres, and the women played it superbly.

If you couldn't reach the ball and a rival player could, you threw your stick at it or her.

If you swung at the ball and missed, you swung again. Whatever you hit, player or ball, it was all the same. If you missed the ball and hit the player, too bad for her. She shouldn't have been in the road anyway.

If you hadn't played the game before and you didn't know what to do when the ball came your way, don't worry about it: just sit on it. Then the referee would blow the whistle and the game would start again.

Not to worry if you got hit yourself. Just remember who it was who hit you and, some time later in the game, hit her back.

See? It was an easy game.

'This isn't hockey,' Jerry said. 'Look at that girl! She's standing way off side.'

'Oh, that's all right,' I answered. 'She's from Waituhi. Nani Kepa is refereeing this game. He's from Waituhi too.'

'But that's favouritism!'

'No it isn't. That other team won last year. It wouldn't be fair...'

'I know,' Jerry sighed, '...if they win again this year!'

'There's another reason,' I added. 'Nani Kepa actually can't see without his glasses. Wasn't that clever of Nani Marama? I tell you, Waituhi people are cunning as.' I laughed and patted Jerry on the shoulder. 'It's always like this at the beginning, Jerry. After the first rounds are over only the good teams are left, the ones who have really come here to play hockey. As for the rest, well, they've come not just because the game's important but because coming is important. Coming, meeting together, laughing together, having fun together, remembering our family ties, that's what the tournaments are all about. We have to make the most of these few days we have because, afterwards, it's back to work, back to life. Back to—'

Yes, Dad, sometimes I do lose track of who I am and what I am. Pakeha life is so seductive.

At that moment there was a roar from the crowd. The opposing team were approaching the Waituhi goal. Alarmed, Nani Marama yelled out to Nani Kepa:

'Kepa? Hoi, Kepa! You better stop that girl, or else you're sleeping in the cowshed tonight.'

What else was Nani Kepa to do? After all, Nani Marama was his honeybun. He blew the whistle. 'Offside,' he said.

The Waituhi supporters cheered and laughed. The other side started to remonstrate. But Nani Kepa was unmoved. He ordered a penalty hit for Waituhi. Cissie slammed the ball and it sped down the field. Huria picked it up, saw Moana standing in the opposing team's circle, and lifted the ball to her.

However, one of the fullbacks fell on it and wouldn't get up.

'Oh, Auntie, please get off the ball,' Moana yelled.

'Nope,' the woman answered. 'And if you hit me, Moana, I'll tell your mother.'

Other women crowded around. Nani Kepa tried to get through to see what was going on. One of the Waituhi women tripped him up—and while he was otherwise occupied, Moana reached under her auntie, picked up the ball with her hands and threw it into the goal.

'Goal!' Cissie cried.

Nani Kepa got up. What was that? Where was the ball? Oh, was that it in the other side's goal? How did it get there!

'Goal,' Nani Kepa confirmed.

This time, a really huge argument began. The coach for the other side came running onto the field to eyeball Nani Kepa. Laughing, Moana and the Waituhi team came back to the middle of the field to wait out the commotion. She looked at Jerry. He looked at her.

'Great goal,' he said.

'Thank you for letting me use your hockey stick,' Moana answered.

'You might even win,' Jerry smiled.

Moana's eyes twinkled. 'Does that really matter?' she asked.

Then Dad was there. 'Well, son, we've made it through to another year,' he said.

I thought of my kuia, Miro, and how she had begun the tournament as a way of keeping up our tribal links, one village with the others. You know: the family that plays together stays together. And what's going to happen when it's Dad's turn to go and the sky falls down?

Even so, I smiled at Dad.

'Yes, Dad,' I answered.

BEGINNING OF THE TOURNAMENT

Most of the stories in *Pounamu Pounamu* are set in Waituhi. I was twenty-five in 1969 when I began writing them, after reading a comment by Bill Pearson in a book edited by Erik Schwimmer, *The Maori People in the Nineteen-Sixties: A Symposium* (1968), that there were as yet no Maori novelists; I decided to give it a go by practising on short stories first.

It was Nani Mini herself who complained when I told her that I had a dilemma – whether or not to give a fictional name to Waituhi, because that would mean that I would have more creative freedom: I wouldn't have to stick to the correct physical details, think about the whakapapa (genealogy) for my characters, and so on. It was for the protection of Waituhi too, I explained, because there were only around fifty families living there at the time and I didn't want them to be exposed. She really gave me what-for. 'Aren't you proud of Waituhi? Are you ashamed of us?' Although I finally agreed with her, I did shift her house in the stories to a space where I could disconnect it from the reality. And I did rename the characters I was writing about: for instance, Nani Mini is Nani Miro in the stories. I was quite prepared to share Nani Miro with a reading public, but Nani Mini was mine.

Waituhi, even in 1969, was still a great tribal centre for Te Whanau a Kai, my father's iwi. It was a well-known Ringatu stronghold, centred on the painted meeting house Rongopai, although none of this dimension exists in the stories – that was to come later in my career. Waituhi was also a centre of cultural competitions and, of course, Maori sporting competitions like hockey. One of my other grandmothers, Nani Teria (she was my 'real' grandmother, my father's mother, and one of the inspirations for Riripeti in *The Matriarch)* and her husband Perapunahamoa, plus Nani Mini, Nani George and many others, decided to set up the Maori hockey tournaments on the East Coast at the urging of the great Sir Apirana Ngata. He felt that sport was one way of maintaining all the links between the many small kainga of Poverty Bay and the East Coast. In their heyday, the tournaments attracted between thirty and forty teams and over 500 people. They were huge, boisterous, with lots of kai and dances; and, of course, Ta Api must have known that the tournaments would also encourage unity in other ways ... like young men and women from different hockey teams getting married sooner or later.

This story is one that people like to think of as quintessential Ihimaera. In my deck of cards, it showed that I had a strong suit in humour and knockabout comedy, not always something that writers can do. And by the time I came to writing as a career, having that one foot in one culture and the other in another had given me sufficient distance to be able to 'see' Waituhi – but through the eyes of the outsider, Jerry.

The story came about when I was at the University of Auckland. Dad rang me up to come home to play in that year's hockey tournament. The Waituhi team, he said, was short of players. He asked me to bring a friend along, and

I took Billy, who became Jerry in the story.

THE MAKUTU ON MRS JONES

Here I am, sitting on the couch looking at my toenails, and suddenly I've remembered Mrs Jones. My wife has kicked me out of the bedroom until I've cut my toenails. I must admit that they are long—I haven't cut them for over two months and they're curling over the edges of my feet. It's a shame to cut them though. If I grow them a bit longer, I'll be able to swing on them. But I better cut them. My wife mightn't let me back into bed.

Mind you, it's my own fault that I got caught out. If I hadn't undressed so far away from the bed, she mightn't have seen them. When her eyes grew wide with amazement, I'd thought it was a compliment. She'd backed away, a picture of typical feminine defencelessness and I'd advanced and...

'Get away from me with those claws!' she'd screamed. 'Get away, get away!'

They don't look like claws to me. Boy, anybody would think it was a crime having long toenails. But I'd better get started on them. It's cold in this sitting room. Here goes.

As I said before, looking at my toenails has reminded me of Mrs Jones and the makutu that was put on her by Mr Hohepa. Makutu is what you would call a magic spell, and Maori people believe that if a person gets a bit of you—it might be some hair, a hanky, even a piece of toenail—he'll be able to put a spell on you. A makutu. I'd never really believed my mother when she'd warned me always to get rid of my cut hair or toenails myself, to bury them in the garden or burn them, and make sure nobody sees, until I'd actually seen makutu at work. Remembering what happened to Mrs Jones has reminded me to make sure my toenail clippings are hidden safely away. My wife might put a big spell on me.

I was only a young boy when the makutu was put on Mrs Jones. She was a widow, and she had the contract to do the rural delivery in Waituhi. Her husband had been the rural delivery man before he died, and she took over afterwards. Every Monday, Wednesday and Friday, Mrs Jones would get into her van and go to the Gisborne post office to collect the mail for all the farms and houses in the village and surrounding district. She'd also stop off at the bakery, the grocery and the bookshop to pick up the stores and newspapers ordered by the people on her run. Then she'd start out, stopping at one farm after another, making her deliveries. It was a long job and sometimes it was a heavy one: she often had to take bags of flour or sugar, or heavy farm machinery, to deliver to a person on her round.

But Mrs Jones was a strong woman, and she used to say it was the Irish in her that made her so strong. She was tall too, and quite able to look after herself. She'd still been in her thirties when her husband had died, and the men hadn't even let him be dead a respectable time before they'd started making a play for her. But she wouldn't have any of them on and, if they got too close, they'd find a fist in their way.

She didn't mind a mild flirt, but anything more really got her blood up. The trouble was that she was such a damned handsome woman and had so much spirit, that men found her irresistible. Maybe it was the combination of reckless green eyes and a throaty chuckle which did it. Especially around Pakowhai pa, she was very popular. But she'd just laugh the men off.

'Go back to your wife, Hepa!'

'If you weren't boozed, I might believe you and take you on, Frank Whatu!'

'I'd eat you for breakfast, lunch and tea, boy!'

Because of her attitude, the women weren't at all jealous of her. They knew she wouldn't tolerate any funny business, and saw behind her bluff and cheekiness to the lonely woman inside. Then too, they knew that her fist would always save her.

But even her fist, with all its power, couldn't save her against Mr Hohepa.

Mr Hohepa was one of the men on her round. He was an old man, and was a tohunga in our district. When I was a child, and I'd done something wrong, I wouldn't be threatened with some grotesque bogeyman but with Mr Hohepa.

'Pae kare! I'll put Mr Hohepa on you!' Mum would say if I'd been naughty.

My sisters and I were very scared of him. He was the three in one: Dracula, Frankenstein and the Werewolf. On dark nights, we would swap stories about him: how he'd put a spell on Kararaina Baker and she'd had a baby, or how evil things happened at his house. As the night grew longer, the stories would grow wilder until one of us would begin to cry. Once one of us started, then the rest would, and Mum would come in and say:

'Hey! What's wrong with you kids! If you don't go to sleep, I'll send you to Mr Hohepa's place!'

That always made matters worse, and we really wouldn't be able to go to sleep then. We'd clutch each other tightly in the dark and in the end, we'd sneak into bed with Mum and Dad. Only with them, would we be safe from Mr Hohepa.

We used to avoid him. All the kids around the pa avoided him. If we saw him coming down the road, we'd back away. Anything not to see those fierce black eyes. He'd only have to look at us and we'd think: makutu ... makutu ... If he hadn't been so fearsome looking, I suppose we'd have laughed off the threats of our parents. They didn't seem to be scared of him and they even called him by his first name. We used to think they were very brave. But we'd tremble too, wondering whether Mr Hohepa would strike them down with lightning, or worse still, whether he'd change them into a kina which he would eat later.

I suppose he must have always looked old, even when he was young. Even today, he doesn't seem to have changed in appearance. He was a tall man with an enormous nose which hung over his mouth. His lips were dark purple and were always quivering. We children used to think he was muttering spells—his lips had to be quivering for some reason! His face was very flabby and his eyes were wide and black, with the whites so white that you could tell a mile off when he was coming. One of his ears had a chewed-up look, as if he'd been in a fight during a time when he was a werewolf. From the other ear, hung a long greenstone pendant.

Although he was tall, Mr Hohepa appeared short as he had a stoop because of his bad leg. He had a carved tokotoko stick to help him walk. As children, we were always scared of that tokotoko because it was inlaid with paua which looked like the eyes of people he had possessed. And every now and then, he would mutter to the stick and bang it on the ground as if he were angry with it. Or else he would wave it round his head while he was talking to somebody flat out in Maori. We'd listen, tremble and think:

'Here it comes. The makutu.'

Wherever he went, he always wore a feather cloak. And because he was a tohunga, he was often asked to represent our village at Pakeha functions, like when the library was opened in the nearby city. Pakehas were scared of Mr Hohepa too. The Mayor didn't even say a word when Mr Hohepa got up at a public function and started waving his tokotoko at him because he'd put Mr Hohepa in the second row.

He wasn't married, Mr Hohepa, and we children weren't at all surprised. He was nearing fifty when he put the makutu on Mrs Jones.

That was about twelve years ago. I'm a grown man now, and I realise my view of Mr Hohepa was childish. At the time all I saw of him was his scary qualities. I hadn't understood that the way he dressed, intimidated people and wielded his walking stick were also signs not of makutu but of leadership. Not only was he a tohunga, he was also a very powerful tribal leader. He was like Miro Mananui, who was a tribal leader also and, like her, he was battling to get the Government to give us back our land.

But in those days I was a know-nothing eleven-year-old. I wasn't a very strong kid and had lost more fights than any other boy at school. I remember it was coming on to Christmas at the time, and I needed some money to buy presents for the family and a water pistol for myself.

That's why I went into Mr Anderson's shop when I saw the notice outside:

WANTED
Strong boy to help deliveries

When I saw some of my other friends waiting in the shop, I didn't think I'd have much chance for the job. But I sat down on the stool with them. I'd nothing better to do, and if I went home, Mum would only make me work round the house.

'What's the job?' I asked Winti Edwards.

He shrugged his shoulders.

'Search me,' he said. 'But the notice says they want a *strong* fella.'

'I'm not here for the job,' I told him hastily, making a quick decision. I'd already had one hiding from Winti that week and didn't want another.

'What you here for then?' the others asked.

'Nothing,' I answered. 'I'm allowed to sit here if I want to. You fellas don't own this seat.'

The boys eyed me ominously. Then Winti said:

'Well, you might as well clear off, and you other fellas too, because I'm the only strong one here.'

And to prove it, he crooked his arm, making his muscles swell like growing peaches.

'See?' he growled at me, thrusting the peaches under my nose. 'Have a feel of them!'

I touched them gingerly, afraid that they might hit me in the eye. But before they could do that, Mr Anderson came out of the back room of his store.

'What's the job, boss?' Winti asked, in what he assumed was a manly voice.

'Ask the lady,' he snapped. He pointed to Mrs Jones, who'd been eyeing us all from the counter. Her eyes were twinkling and she was grinning broadly.

'My, what a strong bunch of boys,' she said. 'But I can only have one of you marvellous specimens so ... eeny meeny miney mo, I pick one, the others go. And the one I pick is...' Her finger bounced from one head to the next, up and down the line, almost stopping, then returning, then moving on, wavering, and then...

'Him,' she announced.

'Him?' the others gasped.

'Who?' I gasped.

'Him,' Mrs Jones said again. And she waved me over and got me busy straight away taking the stores out to her van.

I couldn't believe it! I'd got a job!

'Anyway, who wants to work for a woman!' Winti said as he walked out.

'Yeah,' the others chorused.

But I didn't care about them. Afterwards, I asked Mrs Jones why she'd picked me.

'I like losers,' she answered enigmatically. 'I'm one myself.'

I got to know Mrs Jones very well during those long delivery trips. I even fell in love with her. She was a strange woman, laughing one minute and sad the next. Sometimes bursting into a song, then swearing. She had a silent mood as well. When she was in this mood, she drove very quickly, as if trying to leave her thoughts far behind her. The dust would churn thickly behind us, and at every stop, it would catch up like her thoughts and she would be very hard on me.

'Make it snappy, Tawhai.'

'Tawhai, hurry up. There's lots more deliveries to be done.'

'Come on, boy! Move!'

Sometimes her thoughts would make her voice smoulder and she would be unapproachable. I learnt this mood well and left her alone when it came upon her. And after it had gone away, I knew she wouldn't say she was sorry for treating me so badly. She was very proud: 'I'm sorry' wasn't in her vocabulary. But I could tell, from the slow closing of her eyelids and sudden softening of her face, that she was conveying to me what she couldn't put into words.

Otherwise, Mrs Jones was a generous and kind woman. I also thought that she was very clever and often wished I was quick enough to catch her wit. Mrs Jones was famous for her wit. She had a silver tongue, often playful, but also slightly barbed so that you sometimes couldn't tell whether she was joking or not. The tone of her voice conveyed a thousand different meanings to every witty phrase she said. It could be mocking and teasing at the same time. Along with her fist, it was her other main defence against what she used to call 'the wicked wiles of men'.

It was her voice and the sharp way in which she often used it, which brought her into conflict with Mr Hohepa.

Even before I was born, it was customary that all Mr Hohepa's mail and stores were delivered right at his doorstep. From what I've heard, it took him a long time to establish this privilege. Usually, rural mail isn't delivered right to the house. Farm houses are generally too far off the road to make it practicable. But Mr Hohepa was convinced he was a special case. He was a tohunga, after all. He'd written to the Postmaster-General, the Minister of Maori Affairs, the Minister of Transport, but they, courageous people, had refused his request. However, he'd got his own back, by makutu it is reputed, when that particular Government changed the next year. But even the following Government wouldn't do anything for him, despite his helping them to power, so he'd seen the Mayor. The Mayor referred Mr Hohepa to the local County Council, who politely asked the mail contractors to 'let the old boy have his way, just to keep him happy!' Although they had baulked at first, the mail contractors finally accepted the polite request and that was when Mr Hohepa's mail began to be delivered right to his door. There he would be, sitting on the verandah like a king, acknowledging the service with a grunt and one tap of his tokotoko stick on the floor. Two taps meant: Wait, there is something to be taken back to town. Three taps meant: You are now dismissed. And sometimes he would tap sharply four times if you left in seeming disrespect. So you returned and he looked you over disdainfully before tapping three times again.

Mrs Jones thought him insufferable. She said it was too much to be expected to open and close three gates to get to his place, and then open and close them again to get out. Servility was not in her character. What grated even more was the fact that Mr Hohepa made you feel so common, as if he were royalty and you were one of his lowest subjects. Mr Hohepa knew a rebel when he saw one. During the first few rounds I was with Mrs Jones, he taunted her with his silent disdain. One day, he went too far.

That particular day, Mrs Jones was in one of her moods, only this time it seemed to issue from her and create whirlwinds along the road. The trees bent, the tall grass swayed violently and the dust swept along with the van. Mrs Jones drove so fast that the bends of the road leapt at us like gloves being thrown in our faces. I couldn't do anything fast enough that day. I did my best though, and kept silent, staring straight ahead at the unwinding road and not at Mrs Jones' grim face. By the time we arrived at Mr Hohepa's place, her mood was at its peak. It was unfortunate that that day Mr Hohepa had a huge carton of legal papers being delivered to him—no doubt concerning one of the court cases he and Miro Mananui had about our land—as well as his usual bag of flour, bag of sugar, other stores and his newspapers. Had it been a small delivery, nothing might have happened.

The van sprang at the first gate. I opened and closed it, and then ran to the second gate where Mrs Jones had driven the van. As she went through I could feel the whirlwind whistling around me. The next gate was much further away, so Mrs Jones waited for me and I jumped on the running board. I could see her hands gripping the steering wheel tightly. At the last gate, while I was waiting for the van to go through, Mrs Jones was lighting a cigarette when I suddenly saw her eyes flash like lightning from a black cloud. She threw the cigarette away and stared straight to where Mr Hohepa was waiting, his hands folded over his lap, sitting in his rocking chair on the verandah. As I jumped back into the van, her quiet whisper exploded around me.

'I'll show him!'

We drove quickly up to the house. Some of Mr Hohepa's hens, almost as proud as he was, were wandering across the track, quite sure that the van would stop and wait until they had reached the other side. They scattered and squawked loudly, and flapped away, outraged, as the van careered through their midst. Mr Hohepa saw all this, and his face stiffened. But he didn't say a word—not then, anyway.

I jumped down from the van and opened the back. The carton wasn't too heavy. I carried it up the steps and waited for instructions. The tokotoko made a wide sweep and ended pointing at the door. I laid the carton to one side of it and went back for the bag of sugar. This too, by royal decree, was to be placed near the door. All this time, Mr Hohepa didn't even look my way. He was too busy disdainfully eyeing Mrs Jones.

It was while I was carrying the bag of flour up the steps that it happened. I slipped and the bag fell. I waited for Mrs Jones to tell me off. She yelled all right. But not at me.

'Well, don't just sit there as if you owned the world, Hohepa! Help the boy!'

Mr Hohepa's eyebrows arched. Then he sniffed and tilted his chin a little higher in the air.

And me? Was I scared? Was I what. I'd never heard anybody call Mr Hohepa by his surname alone.

Mrs Jones got out of the van. She slammed the door. Grimly, she took one end of the bag and helped me drag it onto the verandah. Then she looked at Mr Hohepa with disgust and went back down the steps.

The tokotoko drummed on the floor. Four sharp taps. I trembled. I saw Mr Hohepa level a gaze at Mrs Jones and give a challenging smile. Then his tokotoko circled in the air and began jabbing at the door. He wanted us to take the bag of flour right into his kitchen.

Mrs Jones swore under her breath.

Again the tokotoko circled and jabbed at the door. Hurriedly, I went to do as Mr Hohepa commanded but the tokotoko motioned me away and then pointed at Mrs Jones. She was the one who was to do it. And she was to do it alone.

'Like hell I will!' Mrs Jones yelled and her words cracked the air. She tossed her head and took another step from the verandah.

The tokotoko banged away again. Mr Hohepa's rage was terrible to behold. I trembled and thought: here it comes

... the makutu. Fearfully I watched as Mr Hohepa and Mrs Jones fought silently and grimly for domination over the other. It seemed a battle between giants. The air was tense with hostility. They faced each other, it seemed, while decades and centuries whirled past. And then Mrs Jones smiled.

'Take it in yourself,' she said calmly.

She showed her back to Mr Hohepa and he stood up, shivering with anger.

'You! Woman! You dare to...'

But he didn't get any further, for Mrs Jones interrupted him with a hail of words. She must have been spoiling for a fight with him for a long time. Sitting up there like a king! she said. She knew, she said, she knew all about him. Thought he was just the cat's whiskers, didn't he! Thought he was something in this district, didn't he! Well, she knew better. He was too big for his boots, that was his trouble. And he needn't start swearing at her in Maori, either. She knew what he was saying. Yes, thought he was just royalty, didn't he! Everybody knew, she said, that he was just common. He didn't really have any authority around here. Just because his mother had been an ariki didn't make him one. Well, she wasn't going to kiss his common behind. And, she said, things were going to be different from now on!

I listened to them quarrelling: Mr Hohepa raging away in Maori and shaking his tokotoko in the air; Mrs Jones, barking like a small terrier. I edged away from them and sneaked into the van. Every now and then, I'd take a peep at Mr Hohepa. He was almost purple, and his voice blasted out like a trumpet.

'Don't you talk to me like that!' he said. 'I warn you, woman! You're just a public servant. I'll report you,' he said. 'Yes, they'll listen to me. Coming here and disturbing my peace. Running down my hens. Yes, I saw you, woman,' he said. 'I saw you! And don't you answer me back either. So much talk, your husband must have died of it!'

Mrs Jones didn't take that lying down. She launched into the attack again.

'Report me, go on, report me!' she yelled. 'See if I care! And don't you dare talk like that about my husband. He loved me, which is more than anyone can say about you. They all laugh at you, yes, they laugh at you, sitting up here in all your pomp and splendour. You should see yourself! God, if ever I was to marry again and you were the last man on earth, I wouldn't even look at you!'

And with that blistering remark, she turned away from him and stepped into the van. All the time, Mr Hohepa was still yelling from his verandah, banging away with his stick.

'Pae kare, woman!' he said. 'I warn you, you better do as I say. This flour, you come back and take it inside. You just do as I tell you!'

And he began to mutter what seemed to be a magic spell. I looked at Mrs Jones; she was in for it now. But she just laughed, started the van, put her foot down, and we roared away from the verandah toward the first gate.

'Leave it open!' she yelled to me. I hesitated, and looked back to where Mr Hohepa was still yelling and jumping around.

'Leave it open, I say!' Mrs Jones ordered again.

So I did. That gate, the second and the third. And as we turned off down the road, Mrs Jones waved her hand and tooted her horn at Mr Hohepa.

'That'll show him!' she said to me. 'Let him shut his own gates!'

I was horrified. Didn't Mrs Jones know that she was doing something dangerous? Her cheeks were flushed and her eyes were sparkling with triumph.

'He hasn't seen anything yet!' she said. Then she laughed, a long laugh which bubbled in the air. I looked at her amazed, and if I had had any doubts about whether I really loved her, they were dispelled right there and then. I'd never seen Mrs Jones look so beautiful.

That was just the beginning.

On the next round, we left Mr Hohepa's stores at the third gate.

The round after that, his stores were left at the second gate.

On the third round, just inside the first gate.

And on the fourth, Mr Hohepa's stores were deposited on the side of the road.

And always, Mrs Jones would wave and beep the horn at Mr Hohepa before leaving, and I would see his eyes glowing from the shadow of the verandah.

Around this time, I was thinking of resigning from my job. It was getting unhealthy. Makutu ... makutu ... Only my love for Mrs Jones persuaded me to stay.

Naturally, everybody soon found out what was happening. Most of them were on Mrs Jones' side, but admitted a healthy respect for Mr Hohepa. I became one of the most popular people around. I'd be asked:

'What happened today, Tawhai?'

And I'd have to tell them the same story: that we'd just delivered Mr Hohepa's stores to the first gate and no farther.

'But what happened?' they would ask again, impatiently. 'Surely there's something else! You must be hiding something, that's why you're scared to tell us, eh. Mr Hohepa put a makutu on Mrs Jones, eh? You don't have to hide anything. We won't tell!'

In the end, I used to manufacture a story to satisfy them. I'd dwell at length on the fierce countenance of Mr Hohepa. How he'd come running up the road, shouting curses at Mrs Jones, and how Mrs Jones had shouted back at him. Anything, just to have some peace from all those Jack Nohis who wanted to know every little detail. I must admit that I enjoyed it, but even so I began to feel more uneasy. And in one of my more sane moments, I said to Winti Edwards:

'Hey! Do you want my job? You can have it if you like.'

He just laughed at me.

'You can keep your harateke job!'

Around that same time, Mrs Jones' boss on the Council also found out what had happened. One day, when we were almost ready to set off on our round, he came to see her. He was very worried.

'Mrs Jones,' he said, 'I've heard that you've been having a bit of trouble.'

'No,' Mrs Jones answered innocently. 'Not as far as I know.'

The Council man coughed, embarrassed.

'Well,' he continued, 'I've heard, only heard mind you, that you and Mr Hohepa have ... well ... that you haven't been delivering his stores to his door.'

Mrs Jones flared.

'Did he tell you that?'

'Oh, no,' the Council man interrupted hastily. 'I've just heard about it. I don't know whether it's true or not, but I'd just like to say that Mr Hohepa is a very powerful man and...'

Mrs Jones cut him short.

'Don't you worry about me!' she snapped. 'I can look after myself.'

The Council man looked at her and then nodded.

'I suppose you can,' he muttered. 'But if anything happens to you, the Council disclaims any responsibility.'

Then he walked away. Mrs Jones watched him go, a thoughtful look on her face. She whispered something, meant for herself.

'What do you know? Old Hohepa hasn't reported me.'

Then she collected herself.

'And that's the way it should be,' she said grimly. 'This is only between him and myself.'

She drove like the Devil that day.

Christmas came and went. I saw the old year out and the new year in. I bought my water pistol. Rural deliveries were discontinued over the holidays. It was a happy time, and yet I couldn't help feeling worried about Mrs Jones. I was sure that something would happen to her. Something to do with makutu. Something. And not even the fact that Mr Hohepa had smiled at her on Christmas Eve when they'd met in the pub, could dispel my fears.

That night, Mrs Jones had decided to have a drink before going home. One gin had led to another and she'd remained at the bar, laughing and talking with the farmers and their wives. They'd all been congratulating her about the way she'd finally gotten the best of old Hohepa, when he'd walked in.

Silence had fallen quickly. The people surrounding her had drawn away, just like they do in cowboy pictures when there's a shoot-out. Their eyes had glistened with fear, yet also with excitement.

I'd been outside the pub at the time. But as soon as I'd seen old Hohepa go in, I'd run to the window to see what would happen. I remember it, even now.

Mr Hohepa walked slowly to the bar.

'Two flagons of beer,' he ordered.

The barkeeper edged away, felt under the bar and hoisted out two flagons.

Mr Hohepa paid for them. Then he turned.

His eyes locked on Mrs Jones. A queer look came into them as he surveyed her.

She looked like the beautiful saloon girl of countless western films. She was an oasis in a desert. If she had been a pool of water, she would have been drunk dry. Just looking at her made you feel thirsty. Her beauty was almost unbelievable. She was the world's desire and she sat there, alone at the bar, swinging a foot and holding her glass to her cheek. Lucky glass, to touch the cheek of Mrs Jones!

Then she sighed, a long, languid sigh which breathed soft perfume on the air.

'Have a drink with me, Hohepa.'

Nobody moved, but everywhere, eyebrows lifted to the ceiling.

'Let's have a truce over Christmas,' she continued.

Mr Hohepa didn't answer. He just kept looking at her, with that strange look in his eyes. Then he smiled.

That smile. It grew slowly on his lips, arching into a grin, then slowly lowering and closing.

'A truce, Hohepa?'

Still he was silent. Then with a brief nod, he picked up his flagons and left the hotel, his tokotoko tapping softly after him.

The noise returned like an explosion. The people in the pub crowded around Mrs Jones, marvelling at her coolness.

'That'll show old Hohepa!' someone laughed.

I wasn't so sure. That smile. And that wheezy laughter. I can almost hear Mr Hohepa chuckling to himself as he did that night when he passed me in the dark.

Ah! Almost finished my toenails now. Three more to go, and then maybe I'll be allowed back into bed. I don't know why my wife insists on my cutting them. They protect my feet. Against hers.

Anyway, to get back to Mrs Jones and Mr Hohepa.

After New Year, the feud was resumed. We still left Mr Hohepa's stores at his first gate; he was always watching from his verandah. Round after round, it was the same story, and I almost began to believe that Mrs Jones was safe and that Mr Hohepa would make no reprisals against her.

Then a registered letter came from the Minister of Maori Affairs, addressed to Mr Hohepa, which we'd have to take right to his house so that he could sign the receipt for it.

Mrs Jones' fury knew no bounds. She stamped about the post office arguing with the postmaster, and would have torn out her hair if she weren't so vain about it. Couldn't Hohepa come to the post office to get the letter? Or couldn't she just leave it at the gate with the rest of his stores? No, she had to deliver it into his hands. It was in the regulations.

Mrs Jones was still furious when we started off that day. She kept saying she wasn't going to deliver it to him personally, she just wasn't. But as we neared his place, her temper calmed and her eyes twinkled. By the time we arrived at his house she'd accepted her fate.

'It'll be worth it, just to see how the old boy's standing up against the siege,' she said.

As usual, Mr Hohepa was sitting on his verandah, like a big black cat sunning himself. He must have been startled when he saw the van coming right to his house. By the time we'd drawn up to the verandah, a big smile of satisfaction and triumph had spread across his face.

'For you,' Mrs Jones said, snapping out the words. 'Sign here.'

The transaction took place in a tense atmosphere. Mr Hohepa took his time over signing for the letter. Then it was done. Mrs Jones turned to go.

The tokotoko tapped four times.

Mrs Jones looked at him swiftly, her anger brimming. But before she could say anything, Mr Hohepa opened his arms and said:

'Woman, have a drink with me.'

I couldn't believe it! Neither could Mrs Jones. Then the astonished look dropped away from her face.

'Are you asking me or telling me?' she asked angrily.

'Asking you, woman,' Mr Hohepa replied. 'Come.' He motioned to the house. 'Come.'

Mrs Jones stood there a moment, a look of distrust on her face. Then she laughed and said:

'I don't mind if I do, Mr Hohepa!'

She beckoned me to follow her, but I stood my ground.

'I'm not thirsty,' I said. 'I'll just wait out here.' I didn't want to go inside because I was scared I might never see the daylight again. Anyway, if anything happened to Mrs Jones, I wanted to be able to get help. I didn't like the way old Hohepa was looking at her with that funny gleam in his eye. I wanted to caution her, but she just winked at me and went in before I could say anything.

I don't know what happened inside that house. Thinking back, I wished I had gone with Mrs Jones. Maybe I would have been able to save her. As it was, I remained in the sunlight, my fears bursting around me. I heard them talking in there, then silence, an exclamation, then a giggle. Then silence came again, and there was only the noise of the hens pecking at my feet because my toenails must have looked like maize. I felt like running in and dragging Mrs Jones away and had almost plucked up the courage to do so when she appeared. Her face was very straight, as if she were trying to hide something. She didn't speak to me. She simply motioned me to the van. Mr Hohepa came to the doorway to watch us go, and his eyes, they were shining brilliantly. He didn't wave; she didn't say goodbye. She just started the car and we departed. But I knew something had happened in there. Mrs Jones, she had changed somehow.

And when she later remarked that she'd lost her hanky somewhere, my worst fears were confirmed. For, as we'd been leaving, I'd seen the tip of a hanky protruding from Mr Hohepa's pocket. He had something belonging to Mrs Jones. All he needed to do was to cast a spell on it, and she would be in his power.

Makutu.

I tried to keep the knowledge to myself. But the days went by and Mrs Jones did begin to change. At first, the change was almost imperceptible. A slight shivering whenever we went past Mr Hohepa's place. A sudden darting of her eyes toward that shadow on the verandah. Then, the change became more noticeable: Mrs Jones' eyes began to be filled with a fevered look. Her laughter became more brittle, her manner more wild. Her moods kept changing so rapidly, that I could never keep up with them. And I often discovered her staring into the distance, as if at some invisible face.

Mr Hohepa was asserting his power. It was getting stronger and stronger. And Mrs Jones, she was going to the pack.

In the end, I couldn't bear it. I had to find some way to rescue Mrs Jones! I couldn't stand by and see the love of my life being slowly snuffed out. So I confided in Mum.

'Mum, Mr Hohepa's got a hanky of Mrs Jones.'

'Aaaaa!' Mum sighed.

'Mum! I've got to do something!' I said desperately.

'Nothing you can do, Tawhai,' Mum answered. 'Nobody can do anything. Not unless you can get that hanky back. But even then, maybe it's too late. Maybe Mrs Jones is already too much in Mr Hohepa's power.'

Nevertheless I thought I'd try anyway. I had to do something! Even if it did mean entering Mr Hohepa's house.

One dark night, I went out there. The moreporks were hooting and circling around the house. The clouds were dark demons hovering in the sky. I prayed to God and tried to still my heart.

The lights were shining in the sitting room. Mr Hohepa was still up. I made my way round to the back door. It wasn't locked. But I kicked something.

'Who's out there?' a voice yelled.

'Miiaaow,' I answered.

No footsteps came. But I clung to the shadows for a long time, not daring to move. Then I sneaked inside.

I'm not a brave person in any circumstances. As I said before, I was always getting a hiding. So I must have really been in love with Mrs Jones to do what I did that night!

First, I looked in Mr Hohepa's bedroom. My heart sank at the sight of it: there was so much junk in the room that it would be impossible to find one handkerchief. But, I reasoned, it must be somewhere obvious, probably in some kind of sacred place where he cast his spells. All I had to do was look for a place which looked sacred.

There seemed none in the bedroom. So I crept back along the corridor. It was then that the door to the sitting room opened. I had just enough time to hide before Mr Hohepa came out. He stood at the door and then his voice rang out:

'Stay!'

But he wasn't addressing me. He was addressing the person who was with him. It was Mrs Jones, sitting in a chair, a dazed look upon her face.

I had come too late.

Soon after that, school started again, and I had to quit my job. It was a relief in a way as I couldn't bear to see Mrs Jones changing so much. She became thinner, and her personality seemed subdued. She hardly laughed. And once, when somebody said something against Mr Hohepa, she sprang to his defence like a cat spitting and snarling.

I never saw her much after that. I avoided her if I could, mostly because I had failed her. By then, everybody knew what was happening; that the makutu had been put on Mrs Jones, so no matter where I went, I always heard the latest about her. And at each report, she seemed to be getting worse, until finally she was broken.

Well, that's my toenails done. Now I better gather them up and hide them. There's great power in makutu.

Yes, Mr Hohepa got his own way in the end. He won against Mrs Jones. She began delivering his mail to his doorstep as before and she continued to do so until she retired. Old Hohepa, he made sure that Mrs Jones would always be under his will. He was sure cunning, that old fella, I'll have to say that for him. I suppose, because I was in love with Mrs Jones, it's no wonder I was the last to guess that she and Mr Hohepa would get married.

THE MAKUTU ON MRS JONES

Once I had decided to try writing short stories, the ambition kicked in. I had written plot outlines and short paragraphs on the wall of our farm when I was younger. When I was at Gisborne Boys' High, Mr Grono, our English teacher, had awarded me the prize for best short story. And Nani Mini must have told some of her mates that I was writing because I overheard Mrs Waitaiki say to another kuia, 'We'd better stop talking, here comes Witi-Boy Walton.'

Having an interest in writing and being serious about it, however, are two different matters. I realised that I had to get some technical know-how, so in 1970 I enrolled in a short story course run by Barry Mitcalfe in Wellington and, following that, I made it my goal to write one short story a month and try to get them published. Lo and behold, 'The Liar' was accepted by the *New Zealand Listener* on the very day my wife Jane and I were married, 9 May.

One of the subeditors there was author Noel Hilliard who, before they accepted a second story, 'The Child', asked if I would meet him. When I walked into his office he looked at me and gave this huge grin, 'I knew you had to be Maori but, mate, I wanted to make absolutely sure.' He and his wife Kiriwai became great friends and mentors. Kiri worked in Post Office Headquarters sorting mail, and sometimes I would find her handwriting scribbled over my letters, 'Kia ora Witi! Writing?'

'The Makutu on Mrs Jones' truly did begin when Jane kicked me out of bed because my toenails were too long – a story many of her students found dismaying. Of course I shouldn't have had the main character cutting his toenails at night, as my mother, Julia, pointed out to me crossly, because that's a cultural no-no; when the book came out, she was also irritated at some of the linguistic errors, which she said I should have known about. She also didn't like the way I was satirising the concept of makutu.

Mum was one of the people who thought I was writing about the great

Te Kani Te Ua, because there was a story circulating at the time concerning an altercation he was having with the Post Office and the delivery of his mail. The story is about him ... and it isn't.

Larry Parr made a short film of the story, with Annie Whittle playing the postmistress and Sonny Waru as Mr Hohepa.

FIRE ON GREENSTONE

When my Nani Miro died, her husband, my Nani Tama, stayed alone in their old homestead.

The homestead was right next to the meeting house, and set a little back from the road. It was a big house encircled by a verandah. Nani Tama used to sit there alone, basking in the sun. The people of the whanau would often visit him, bringing with them their crates of beer, and they would sing songs and talk about the old days with him. Nani Tama liked that. He would sigh and lean back in the wicker chair and dream. Then his old lips would quiver with emotion, and sometimes he would ramble on about the times gone, and about his wife, my Nani Miro.

'She sure loved her cards,' he would whisper. 'Sometimes, I used to think how good it would've been if only I'd been a King of Clubs. She used to say that the King of Clubs was her lucky charm. Always got her out of trouble, she used to say. I don't know why. I don't know why.' And he would smile to himself, remembering.

Sometimes, remembering made him sad. Then he would grasp his tokotoko, his walking stick, and you would see him shuffling slowly along the road, going through the gate at the bottom of the hill where the graveyard was, and up the slope to where the headstones pricked the skyline. There, beside Nani's grave he would sit, a small black speck, unmoving against the rushing clouds and turning world, talking to Nani as she lay beneath the earth. Then, after a long while, you would see him descending the hill, the emerald sparkling slope, returning to the homestead.

I was waiting for him one afternoon, waiting for him to return. I'd come back home from Wellington on one of my infrequent holidays. From a long way off, I saw him and went to meet him. It had been a year since Nani Miro had been buried on the hill. After I had embraced Nani Tama, he looked up at me and whispered:

'Your Nani was a great lady. All her life she kept Waituhi together. All her life she protected the land we live on and fought to get back the land that was taken away. Who will carry on the work now that she is gone?'

We sat on the verandah for a long time. We talked and laughed together, and we shared a beer.

'Don't tell me you booze now,' he whispered.

'I'm trying to catch up to you,' I answered.

'Boy!' He laughed huskily. 'You'll never catch me up. I drink this stuff like water!'

I elbowed him playfully. 'If Nani Miro was here, she'd soon put a stop to that. Look at you! You're even skinnier than me now, you're turning into a bag of bones.'

He chuckled. Then he beckoned me inside the homestead.

The homestead ... As a small boy, I used to think it was like a palace. The wooden lattice-work fringing the verandah with its curved and whorled designs was like lace decoration. At each corner of the verandah were thin moulded and tapered columns, and the doors had panels of frosted glass in them. The windows too, were set with coloured glass, and I used to like peering out of them and seeing the world made crimson or green or deep, dark blue. From afar off, you saw the homestead like a big white wedding cake, gleaming on a sunny day.

Like everybody else, I called it 'The Museum'. In a way, that's what it was too, and as I followed Nani Tama, I began to look around for the ornaments and pictures with which I'd been so familiar as a child.

In the kitchen, the old newspapers which served as wallpaper were still there, now yellowing and ripped in places by the procession of mokopunas who'd come to stay from time to time. And there, to one side of the safe, was the old newspaper spread which I'd always found fascinating: a report with fading pictures of men and antiquated vehicles on the Western front during the Great War. Above the sideboard, a tarnished silver ornament that my Nani Miro had won when she'd been a young girl, in a roller skating competition of all things!

'Oh, you should have seen me, mokopuna,' she used to say when I went to visit her. 'I could do a lot of tricks on those skates ... and then I met your Nani Tama and he made me have one kid after the other and—' she would sigh '—now the only sport I'm any good at is poker.'

We walked along the short hallway, Nani Tama and I, and he opened the door to the sitting room. The same sensation crept softly over me as I used to feel as a child whenever I saw that room.

This room was the whanau; the whanau was this room. If ever you wanted to know the whanau's accomplishments, here they were all on show. Here were all the sports trophies, shields, photographs of the old people who'd died long ago, whakapapa or genealogy sheets, carved feather boxes, panels, figurines, feather cloaks, piupius—all spilling a riot of colour and shadow throughout the sunlit room. In this room, surrounded by the past and ancestral memories, Nani Miro had presided over meetings with other elders discussing Treaty matters, the politics of the times and the return of the land.

And, on more informal occasions, right in the middle was the big round table where the kuias used to sit with Nani, playing cards. Looking at it, so lonely now, I could almost hear Nani Miro squabbling with Mrs Heta, to see Mrs Heta's one googly eye reaching right across the table to sneak a look at Nani's cards.

'Keep your eyes to yourself, Maka tiko bum! You can cheat all right!'

'You the cheat, Miro Mananui! You the cheat! I saw you sneaking that ace from the bottom of the pack!'

And crammed in one corner, was the old piano that Nani Miro used to like me to play. Whenever some of her younger mokopunas wandered over to it, she would yell: 'You fellas keep your hands off! Only two people are allowed to touch that piano! Me and him!' she'd said, pointing to me. At the time, I'd felt proud that Nani thought me somehow special. But later, my cousins gave me a hiding and said:

'Anyway, who wants to play on that stink piano!'

After that, I didn't like it when Nani Miro used to refer to me when talking about the piano.

I wandered over to it, stepping between the piles of piupius and old clothes.

'It's still open,' Nani Tama said.

I caressed the keys softly. They were all yellow except for one which had had the ivory covering prised off it. I grinned, remembering that my cousin Hirone had done that. He'd seen a film about ivory hunters, gotten it into his head that the keys of a piano were valuable too, and sneaked in to remove one of them. Nani Miro had been real mad when she found out.

My fingers moved across the keys, and began playing a tune. From somewhere far away, I heard an old voice softly singing:

Me he manurere, aue,
Kua rere tito, moenga...

The voice drifted away as I took my hands off the piano and I smiled at my Nani Tama. He nodded wisely. Then we heard a truck draw up outside, and a voice yelling out: 'Tama! Hey, Tama Mananui!'

Nani Tama went out to see who it was, and I was left alone, to wander in the room.

When I'd been a child and bored with watching the old women playing their card games, I used to like wandering through that room, looking at the old photographs and fingering the carvings and the soft sheen of the feather cloaks. I did the same thing now, alone, a year after my Nani Miro had gone away from me.

This photograph: the Waituhi Men's Hockey Team, 1938, and Nani Tama young and tall, holding the winner's shield.

In the glass case on the other side of the room, there was the shield itself, darkly varnished, with rows of shining silver inlaid squares where the names of the winning teams throughout the years were inscribed.

Another sports photograph, and another, and another.

Scattered throughout the room, silver sports trophies, big and small, all shapes and sizes, cups and shields, gleamed in the light.

A big oval photograph, coloured by an artist long ago, of a young woman with the moko tattooed on her chin: that had been my Nani Miro's grandmother and my great-great-grandmother. A handsome woman, wearing a cloak proudly over her shoulders.

Above the fireplace, the cloak itself was draped, still softly glowing with rippling bird feathers. I reached up to touch it, and it was warm and silky to touch. Then my fingers strayed over a small carved figure, following the curves and spiral whorls and feeling the rough edges left by the carver.

Next to the cloak was a piupiu, spread wide across the wall. It swished and crackled and fell coolly around my arms like a waterfall. Beside it, hung two long pois, my Nani Miro's pois, which she used in action song competitions at Takitimu Hall.

In one corner, were the bodice tops, piupius and peruperu spears used by the men in the haka. And I remembered that they would soon be used again—for I had come home for the Maori Hockey tournament and there would be action song competitions during the night.

And on an old table, a photograph of Nani Miro herself, her face creased in a smile and her one black tooth showing. She used to say that if it wasn't for that porangi tooth, she'd have been a film star.

I picked the photograph up and grinned back. Then my eyes fell upon a large book, opened, and showing entries written in different inks by different hands. This held the whakapapa of the whanau, the genealogy of the people of the village. I looked over those names, so familiar, because although these people were dead, they were all my family too. And I saw where Nani Tama had made the last entry: Miro Heremaia Mananui.

Then Nani Tama returned.

'That was Joe Baker,' he told me. 'He brought your Nani some kanga kopiro. You like rotten maize, mokopuna? You want a feed?'

I shook my head.

'No, Nani,' I said. 'I have to go soon.'

He nodded his head. Then his eyes grew serious. He motioned me to a cupboard and brought out a wakahuia, a small carved box.

'You remember this?' he asked.

I nodded. I opened the box. Inside was the greenstone. No one knew how old it was, only that it was very old. When I'd been a young boy, I'd discovered it there and asked Nani Miro if I could have it. But she had growled at me.

'I know you,' she'd said. 'You'd only play war games with it! No mokopuna, not now.'

It was a big piece of greenstone, not the valuable dark green kind, but a smoky green like an opal. But I used to like to hold it to the sun and look into it, and feel the soft luminous glow flooding around me. And I used to whisper to myself, 'Pounamu ... pounamu ... pounamu...', and almost hear the emerald water rushing over the clay from where the greenstone had come.

'Yes, I remember,' I said to Nani Tama, 'I remember.'

That's when Nani Tama looked around the room and asked, 'Shall I give it to him now, Miro?'

For a moment there was silence. Then Nani Tama nodded, turned to me and firmly put the greenstone in my hands.

'Your Nani Miro told me to give this to you when you were ready. Are you ready, Tama? When you are, come home and, this time, stay.'

I went to see Nani Tama again before I left to come back to Wellington.

But one night, the telephone rang for me.

It was Dad and he had bad news. The old homestead, Nani Tama's place, had burned down to the ground that night. Some people had been staying with Nani, and one of them had gone to sleep smoking a cigarette. The blankets had caught fire and the fire had spread quickly through the house. Luckily Nani Tama and the people had been able to get out. But Nani Tama, so Dad said, had gone crazy, looking at the flames and crying:

'Miro! Miro!'

Everybody in the village had rushed to the homestead, bringing buckets, tins and basins full of water. The old people, the young children, all helped, but it was no good. The homestead was old and the flames were hungry upon it. By the time the fire brigade arrived, it was too late. Afterwards a Pakeha had tried to comfort Nani Tama by saying, Never mind. He hadn't understood when Nani had said to him: 'All my family, all this whanau, were in that house. All. And Miro.'

I wept when Dad told me. The homestead wasn't just four walls and rooms. It was the manawa, the heart of the whanau, the heart of the family, and my Nani Tama's heart too. For a long time afterward, I could think only of the flames leaping through the sitting room, licking at the photographs, a sports shield burning, a feather cloak afire, around a table where women used to sit, across an old piano, into a drawer where the whakapapa sheets were kept. But then I remembered the greenstone and Nani Tama's words about carrying on Nani Miro's work. There are some things fire can never destroy. And I saw not fingers of flame but a soft luminous glow reaching out and around me.

FIRE ON GREENSTONE

'Fire on Greenstone' is a kind of sequel to 'A Game of Cards' and is about handsome Nani George Tupara, although in the story he is called Nani Tama. It's the King of Clubs story to go with Nani Mini's Queen of Hearts story. I wasn't much of a card player in those days, nor am I now, but I think that in some card games you have to have what's known as an 'off suit', and if it's not in a red card it's in a black.

The story is set about two years after the fictional Nani Miro has died, but its setting is really Nani Mini's blue house in Waituhi. As I've already said, I loved going to see her whenever I was in Waituhi, and that didn't stop until the day she died. Apart from anything else, The Blue House was where all the feather cloaks, piupiu, trophies and shields were stored. In the story, however, I 'shifted' her house next to the meeting house so that I could make it into something imagined and metaphorical. It is this, imagined, house which burns down. At the time

I was writing the story, the burning down of 'Miro's Museum' was supposed to be symbolic of what I saw was happening to rural Maori culture and tribal continuity. Sometimes I can get too clever: the New Zealand Fire Service asked if they could use the story in a fire prevention campaign directed at Maori.

Throughout 1970 I kept writing my one story a month. I was being supported by a number of people, including Gill Shadbolt (I was working in Post Office public relations in Wellington) and also my dear, wonderful friend Joy Stevenson, editor of *Te Ao Hou,* a magazine of Maori writing, who saw that there was a new kid on the block joining other Maori fiction writers such as Arapera Blank, Riki Erihi, Mason Durie, Katarina Mataira, Patricia Grace and Rowley Habib. I used to sneak into the Wellington Public Library from time to time to look at Jacquie Sturm, but I was too shy to approach her.

Among other supporters was a gentleman by the name of Arthur Jones, then a script editor for the New Zealand Broadcasting Corporation. My good friend Fiona Kidman introduced me to him. I credit Arthur with the directness in my writing: in those days you didn't get much mucking around in my stories. This is because Arthur wanted stories that only took ten minutes maximum to read, so I had to learn how to set up a story fast, get listeners to laugh – or cry – fast, and then get out of the story fast. 'A Game of Cards', 'Beginning of the Tournament', 'Fire on Greenstone' and 'In Search of the Emerald City' were all originally written for radio. I wrote two series of stories, twelve in all, and they were read by George Henare, actor, cuzzie bro and fellow East Coastie.

And Fiona and I, ever since, have been hitched to the same star.

THE OTHER SIDE OF THE FENCE

It is Sunday and the Simmons family have just arrived home from a picnic. They are all pleasantly tired. It has been a beautiful day.

Every Sunday, straight after morning church service, it is a ritual of the Simmons' to drive into the country with a hamper of sandwiches and a picnic spread. They often used to go on picnics in England and they see no reason to discontinue the custom now that they live in New Zealand. For three years now, the street has become accustomed to the sight of the Simmons' old car gaily trundling away from the city. Most of the neighbours are indifferent to this weekly occurrence. But in the house next door to the Simmons house, six little black heads are to be seen peering sadly after the departing car. For the Heremaia children, Sunday is a sad day because the Simmonses have gone away. All day they will be seen roaming around in lost circles, making desultory efforts to play games with one another and usually ending up picking on one another. Around the end of the afternoon, they will be seen sitting on the fence which separates their property from the Simmons house, like six little blackbirds parched by the summer. Waiting, just waiting. Waiting for the Simmonses to return home. They like the Simmonses.

But today, there are no blackbirds perched on the fence. Their house is silent and the backyard is empty. No curious cries greet the Simmons car as it turns into the driveway and stops:

'Did you fellas have a good time?'

'Have you got any sandwiches left over for us, Mrs Simmons?'

'Boy! Wish we could've come with you fellas.'

This time there is silence.

Sally Simmons gets out of the car. The two Simmons children, Mark and Anne, scramble after her.

'Mark, take the picnic basket indoors,' Sally instructs. 'Anne, bring in the rug. And Jack, don't take too long locking the car away. I'll make us all a nice cup of tea.'

Jack Simmons nods. He watches as his wife shepherds the children into the house. Then he drives the car into the garage. Carefully, he locks all the doors of the car. Then he pauses, chuckles to himself, and glances quickly toward the house next door.

And at a bedroom window, he sees little Jimmy Heremaia staring back at him.

Jack Simmons' smile grows broader. He locks the garage door as well. Better to be safe than sorry. There's no telling what those Heremaia kids might get up to next.

Satisfied now, Jack Simmons walks up the path toward his house. He takes off his shoes.

'Sally, have I time for a shower before dinner?'

'Yes, but come and have a cuppa first, dear.'

He goes into the kitchen. Mark and Anne are milling around the biscuit jar. Sally shoos them away. The table is set with two glasses of milk for the children and Sally is preparing a cup of tea for herself and her husband.

'It won't be long. Mark! Anne! To the table, please.'

The children seat themselves. After a while, Mark says:

'I wonder where they are?'

'Who?' Jack Simmons asks.

'George, Henare, Annie...'

'Probably having their dinner,' Sally Simmons answers.

'And hopefully,' Jack Simmons interrupts, 'going straight to bed after their dinner too!'

Sally Simmons playfully nudges her husband. He winks at her. He himself knows it is too much to expect that the Heremaia children would go to bed so early. Heavens, he is lucky that the tribe has not invaded his house yet! He winces to himself. He may as well make the most of these quiet and unassailed moments.

If he were asked, Jack Simmons would never go as far as saying he disliked the Heremaia children. He rather liked them in a hesitant and cautious sort of way. Heavens, he had known very well when he was told his neighbours were Maori, that he would have to expect the worst. People had informed him so, but what the worst was, they had not told him; only that he was to expect it. In his case, the worst turned out to be the Heremaia children. Mind you, they were not always bad children and there were times when he liked them unreservedly. But at other times ... he didn't dislike them really, but he was, he'd have to admit, very wary of them. Their behaviour was so erratic and such a mystery! Sometimes they were pleasant and then unpleasant. Good and then bad. Honest, then dishonest. Generous, then mean. And even though they had received a sound Christian training, their sense of morality seemed to come and go, come and go, with the most astonishing ease. On Sunday mornings, Jack Simmons would watch them walking in single file to church, their faces scrubbed and beaming smiles in the general direction of Heaven, and he would sigh to himself. How could such apparent angels also be such proper little devils! Jack Simmons had long given up trying to understand them.

Take George, the eldest Heremaia boy: eleven years old, a handsome lad, usually courteous and very helpful. George definitely had good traits, but he also had itchy fingers and a tyrannical attitude over children smaller than himself. It was George who had master-minded the last of the raids made by the Heremaia children on Jack Simmons' henhouse. Jack Simmons knew it was George because of the long and colourful feathers he was wearing in one of the interminable games of cowboys and Indians the children in the neighbourhood liked to play. Because George was the roughest and biggest boy in the street, the younger children always tried to get on his side when they played games. Those who weren't, trembled in fear because when George went on the warpath, the cowboys always lost. You could never shoot George; he always refused to stay dead. If he shot you with an arrow, it was better not to argue with him. Otherwise, he'd take you captive and devise horrible tortures for you. Better to groan, clutch at your heart, fall down and suffer your hair to be pulled while

George went through the motions of scalping you.

Henare, a year younger than George, possessed a similar flaw in his character. Like his brother's, it showed itself in the games the children liked to play. Henare was known to all and sundry as The Cheat. No matter what the game, Henare could always be counted on to win it by devious and underhand methods. On one occasion he'd used a marble the size of a pingpong ball to beat Mark in a game of marbles. That was the trouble with both George and Henare: they had no notion whatsoever about fair play. Admittedly Henare had redeemed himself by returning Mark's marbles, but that was because he'd wanted another game and nobody else would play with him. Mark, as usual, lost again.

'Why do you keep playing with him, Mark?' Jack Simmons had asked.

'Because he's my friend!'

'But he cheats you so.'

'He's still my friend. Anyway, he'll soon get tired of playing marbles and then he'll give them all to me. He said he would. He's my friend!'

But these were only incidental flaws, and all the Heremaia children possessed them. Jack Simmons could tolerate them, but there were two traits he would not stand: the curiosity in the Heremaia children which led them to 'borrowing' and then the audacity to deny that they were responsible.

There was the time, for instance, when Jack Simmons had asked them if they knew where his missing bicycle was. He suspected them but every smile and counterfeit tear was designed to prove their innocence; every sigh and gesture expertly tailored to show that they couldn't have done it, not they.

'Mr Simmons, you don't really believe we could have taken it, do you? (Sigh). Oh, Mr Simmons! (Shocked outburst, eyes wide with horror). But we didn't take your bike, truly! (Hands pressed to breasts). Cross our hearts and hope to die if we tell a lie! (And they crossed their hearts too!)'

They were so good at it you felt you had to applaud. They used every body movement and every facial expression that they possessed in their vast and formidable repertoire: rolled eyes, sad-lidded eyes, a tear or two depending on the enormity of the accusation, a couple of long sighs and gurgles, an entreating gesture of the hand, a slight quivering of the lips, more tears if they were necessary, an occasional wail ... and all accompanying the Great Explanation.

'We couldn't have taken your bike today, Mr Simmons, because we went to church. It isn't Sunday? Oh, we remember now, we went down to the river for a swim. We walked all the way too, Mr Simmons, you can ask Mrs Davidson. Has Mrs Davidson really gone away for the weekend? Gosh, some people are lucky! No, it couldn't have been her that saw us then. Well, um, it must have been Mrs Keith. Yes, we walked all the way, true! And Jimmy had a sore leg, too. Show Mr Simmons your sore leg, Jimmy. See? Come to think of it, we did see a boy with a bike like yours down at the river. That's right, and Annie did say: "Hey, you fellas, that looks like Mr Simmons' bike!" But we said to her: "Can't be, because Mr Simmons always locks his bike so we can't pinch it." It must have been your bike, eh, Mr Simmons! If only you'd told us before that it was missing, Mr Simmons. We would have given that boy a good hiding, because you're our best friend. No, we don't know who he was. Never seen him before. Aren't some people awful thieves?'

In this case, despite the grand performance, Jack Simmons' suspicions had proved correct. He'd gone down to the river and found his bicycle together with an eye-witness who'd definitely seen George riding it. So he'd had it out with the children again.

'But we told you we'd taken it, Mr Simmons! Didn't we tell you? We're sure we told you, we all heard each other. See, Mr Simmons, six against one! We're not liars. You're our friend. Oh, no, we didn't steal it. We wouldn't do such a thing. Anyway, you always said we could take your bike when we wanted it. Yes, you did. Can't you remember? Mr Simmons, we all heard you, six against one. So we couldn't have stolen your bike, could we? We just borrowed it and borrowing isn't stealing, is it? No, we won't do it again. Cross our hearts and hope to die if we tell a lie, Mr Simmons! It was only that poor Jimmy here had a sore leg. Not that leg, Stupid! Yeah, and Jimmy fell down and we thought he was crippled. That's why we took your bike. It was an emergency, and you always said that in an emergency we could use your bike. When is Mrs Davidson coming back? Yes, cross our hearts, Mr Simmons. But wasn't it lucky that we took your bike, because if it hadn't been us, bet some other kids would have pinched it. You just left it lying against the fence and Annie said: "We better take Mr Simmons' bike before a thief gets it." That's why we took your bike. Aren't we good?'

Jack Simmons had since come to understand that borrowing was a common Maori trait: what's yours is mine, what's mine is yours. Maybe it was acceptable practice among Maori people but this city suburb was certainly not a Maori community. Things were different now. The land, its occupants and their possessions no longer belonged to them. It belonged to him, Jack Simmons. His land was like the land bought by settlers after the Treaty of Waitangi.

The sooner they understood that, the better.

Jack Simmons hears the sounds of a wire screen door twang open and slam shut. Quickly, he drains his tea. The horde is advancing. He looks out the kitchen window. No, not the horde; only Katarina. Jack Simmons watches as she runs across the backyard and climbs the fence between the two properties. He erected that fence three years ago. Come to think of it, the Heremaia children had helped him build it. Those children, they had no sense of shame whatsoever.

Jack Simmons smiles to himself. The fence might as well not exist. The Heremaia children may have conceded their territorial rights, but not their sovereignty. This they have maintained by the most cunning strategy. Whether the Simmonses like it or not, they have been adopted.

Katarina knocks on the door.

'Come in Katarina!' Jack Simmons yells.

The door swings open and Katarina enters.

'Whew!' she gasps, rolling her eyes. 'I ran all the way and I'm puffed now.'

'Where've you been?' Mark asks her.

'Yes, where?' Anne asks too. 'We thought you'd be over ages ago.'

'Mum's in her mood,' Katarina replies. 'She got mad when we came back. We have to stay inside, but I sneaked out. I can't stay long though.'

Mark and Anne glance at one another. Mrs Heremaia is in one of her moods.

'Hey!' Katarina continues. 'Did you fellas leave any cakes for me? That's what I've come for. You didn't eat everything at your picnic did you?'

'Yes, Katarina, we did,' Jack Simmons replies.

'We did not!' Mark and Anne shout.

'I knew you wouldn't,' Katarina sniffs. 'Eeee! Mr Simmons, you're just having me on. You fellas aren't pigs. You're good to me. We share and share alike, eh.'

Katarina giggles. She watches with bright eyes as Anne brings the left-over cakes to the table.

'Boy!' Katarina says. 'Weren't you fellas hungry? And are those biscuits for me too? But I can't stay. Do you mind? I'll take them with me. I'll give some to Jimmy. He's got the flu or something. Maybe that's why Mum's in her mood. And I'll give some to George, Henare, Annie and Tommy too. Share and share alike, eh!'

'Wait a moment,' Sally says. 'I'll give you a box to put them in.'

'No, it's all right. I'll carry them in my dress. And I promise not to eat them all myself. Gosh, I better go now. But did you fellas have a good time? Wish I could have come with you. Never mind. Anne, I'll give you a yell tomorrow for school. Jimmy's sick. Mum's in her mood. See you! And don't be late tomorrow, Anne.'

Then she is gone.

'Well!' Sally Simmons laughs. 'That child! Here one minute and gone the next!'

'It's your own fault,' Jack Simmons says. 'You shouldn't encourage her with cakes and biscuits. That's all she comes over here for. Every Sunday without fail she comes. I should have stopped it right from the start.'

'Aaah,' Sally laughs. 'But you didn't. Anyway, I like Katarina! She's rather sweet in her own way.'

Sweet? It was not a term that Jack Simmons would generally use to describe any of the Heremaia children. Yet, they were such comic children that you could not always be stern or angry with them. Even if you did dislike them—which Jack Simmons did not—you had to admit that they were at least amusing. Katarina for instance, now she was a comic little girl.

Katarina was affectionately known by her brothers and sisters as Pretty Girl because she was so ugly. Despite this, she had endeared herself to Sally Simmons anyway, from the very start. There had been a knock at the door and Jack Simmons had opened it to be confronted with Katarina in all her radiant ugliness.

'My name is Katarina Makarete Erihapeti Heremaia,' she'd whispered.

Then she'd fluttered her eyelashes and giggled.

'But you can call me Pretty Girl,' she'd continued.

That day, Katarina had wandered through the house as if she owned it. She was the scout among the children. After concluding her inspection she'd walked calmly to the window, put her fingers in her mouth, given an ear-shattering whistle, and the rest of the tribe had come running. They'd never, entirely, in all those three years, been ousted. Least of all, Katarina. She seemed to look upon the Simmons house as her second home.

You could forgive Katarina anything ... except her infuriating curiosity. And then of course, there was the borrowing. Katarina was a veritable magpie. She loved bright things: earrings, shiny beads, little scent bottles, the blue eyes of Anne's doll and money! But Sally had her own way of dealing with Katarina. She would forbid Katarina to come into the house until the missing objects were returned. Katarina idolised Sally. She always returned the missing bright objects. As for money, well, you soon learned not to leave loose change around when Katarina was present.

Annie, the other Heremaia girl, was also rather a character. She was the gasbag of the Heremaia family. She loved talking, and once she had started she just kept on talking ... and talking and talking and talking. She talked so fast and so volubly that sometimes you could never tell where onewordfinishedandanotherword began. You never dared to go out of the house if Annie was wandering out there alone, for she would pounce upon you with great delight and her stream of chatter would issue forth. She was always being scolded about it by her brothers and sisters.

'Who pressed your button?' they would yell at her. 'Who pressed your button, Annie? Who told you to open your big mouth!'

Yes, like her sister, Annie was rather an amusing child. However, there were times when she ceased being amusing and was a downright pest. In common with the other children, she possessed a penchant for borrowing. Loving talking as she did, she was a natural adept at telling long and involved 'stories'. Worst of all, she had a total unconcern for other people's property. The borrowing wasn't nearly as bad as the damage, accidental or otherwise, which Annie could wreak. Branches shattered under Annie, windows tended to break when she was around and a bed of strawberries which Jack Simmons had once cultivated was positively massacred after Annie had been at it. It all seemed amusing in retrospect, but at the time, the incidents had been far from funny. Worse still, you tended to suspect the Heremaia children, because of their record, of *every* misdemeanour which happened. And even if it *was* doubtful whether they had committed it or not, you still felt they must have done it. The goldfish affair was the classic case.

In England, one of Sally Simmons' interests had been the breeding of goldfish. She'd been quite an authority on the subject and had decided to continue her experiments in New Zealand. Jack Simmons constructed a pond for her and she selected certain strains of goldfish which she planned to crossbreed. The result, she hoped, would be a goldfish of a purple colour. Her efforts raised much interest among other breeders and she was considered something of a celebrity in the street. The Heremaia children, especially, used to ask how she was getting on, though they'd been given strict instructions never to go near the goldfish pond. Wire-netting had been stretched across it as an extra safeguard.

After some months, it seemed that Sally Simmons would succeed. She bred a goldfish of a mauve-rose colour. But one morning, the Simmonses awoke to find the wire-netting had been tampered with and that key goldfish was missing. The first thought which came to Jack Simmons was that the Heremaia children had done this terrible thing. A bitter scene followed with Millie and Sam Heremaia. Their children denied taking the goldfish. Finally, as a matter of course, the police were notified. And as a matter of course, they questioned the Heremaia children. This divided the two families even further because Millie and Sam became convinced that Jack

Simmons was out to get at their children. The police never did find the culprit. Relations between the two families were strained for a long time. And Sally Simmons was so upset about the whole affair that she gave up breeding goldfish altogether.

It was an ugly situation and a sad one too. Had the Heremaia children been responsible? They seemed the obvious suspects, the obvious ones to blame. That was the trouble: you thought them guilty even in cases like this one, and you did not give them the benefit of the doubt.

No matter now. The affair had long been over. The Heremaia children had made overtures of friendship and Jack Simmons had accepted them in the end. But the doubt and caution had still remained, dormant perhaps but still there, to feed suspicion against the children when the next crisis flared.

Jack Simmons sighs ruefully. Life next door to the Heremaias has certainly not been a calm one. For three years now, it has continued in a state of amicable warfare, each crisis separated by long periods of amity. If only the Heremaias were a little more balanced in their behaviour! Then relations between the two families wouldn't oscillate in such an extreme manner. Right from the start it has been a series of escalations and deescalations and treaties signed and treaties broken. All very wearing and wearying. Under the circumstances, it is most surprising that the two families have been able to get on at all. Yes, what is needed is a little more stability in the Heremaias. Take Millie now: usually calm and even-tempered, but tonight she is in one of her moods.

'What are you thinking about, Jack?'

Jack Simmons looks up at his wife. She has poured a cup of tea for herself and sits at the table.

'Nothing in particular,' he answers. 'I was wondering about the Heremaias. About Millie.'

'Mrs Heremaia is in her mood,' Mark whispers.

'She's awful when she's in her mood,' Anne continues.

'That's enough!' Sally Simmons interrupts. 'I'd prefer not to hear about

Mrs Heremaia's mood when I'm having a cup of tea, thank you very much!'

Millie's mood is a legend in the street. It is probably not greater than anyone else's raging temper except that when she has it, everybody knows about it. When she is in her mood, you can hear her shouting right at the end of the street. Yet you sometimes find it difficult to believe that she can have such a temper, for she is a small and usually docile woman.

'I wonder why she's in her mood tonight?' Mark asks.

'Who knows?' Jack Simmons replies. 'Mrs Heremaia has her moods for many reasons.'

'That's enough, Jack!' Sally Simmons repeats firmly. 'Or I shall be in one of *my* moods as well!'

Jack Simmons laughs. But he knows that Millie's mood is no laughing matter. Heavens, he has been on the receiving end of it himself. As usual, the incident had been one involving her children. Jack Simmons had merely wanted to ask George if he'd been into the henhouse again, and he'd only touched

George lightly on the arm, just lightly mind you....

And next minute, an angry explosion had sounded from the Heremaia house, the door had almost buckled at the hinges, and Millie had steamed out to rescue her child.

'I saw you, I saw you!' she'd yelled. 'You touched that kid, I saw you doing it with my own two eyes, and don't you tell me that I'm a liar. Not me, boy! You touch him again and I'll lay into you myself, you bully! If you want to pick on somebody, pick on me. I'll show you.'

Jack Simmons takes a hasty sip at his tea. Millie's tirade had kept on and on and had been heard all the way down the street. But Millie didn't care two hoots about that. If people didn't like it, then they shouldn't listen. Nobody was going to lay a hand on her kids and get away with it.

That ghastly episode taught Jack Simmons a very valuable lesson. If you had any accusations to make against the Heremaia children you had to face Millie as well. If your accusations were proven right, you were safe. But Heaven help you if you were wrong. It was best if you meekly joined the queue to see Millie, bearing cap and complaint in hand. And you had to have a good case to present, for Millie had a formidable arsenal of protective motherhood to bring to bear against you.

Yes, if you won your case, you were safe. But you still left Millie in her mood. That was even worse, for Millie was ruthless in punishing her children. Sometimes you wondered whether you should have gone to her at all. Somehow, hearing her punishing her children made you wish you could retrace your steps.

Jack Simmons finishes his cup of tea.

'Are you going to have your shower now?' Sally asks.

'I've changed my mind,' he answers. 'I'll have it after dinner. I'll go down to the henhouse to make sure everything is okay.'

'All right,' Sally Simmons says. 'And you just stop thinking of Millie Heremaia!'

She pushes him out of the kitchen into the passage. Jack Simmons puts on his shoes again.

Strange really, how could you reconcile the Millie Heremaia in her mood with the calm and warm-hearted woman? For that is also Millie Heremaia. Admittedly, she and her husband Sam are not always tactful. Their humour may not always be in the best taste, but it is honest and open. And to hear them laugh is to hear laughter as it really should be: punched straight from the chest with no holds barred. Absurd it may be, but you could say a lot of good about the Heremaias.

Jack Simmons shakes his head, puzzled. He opens the door and goes out of the house. The afternoon is still light and the wind is cool. He looks over the fence at his neighbour's house and is just in time to see Jimmy duck down from the bedroom window. Poor little fellow. Still, he may not have the flu. If only the other children were like Jimmy. If they were, they would cease to be a puzzlement.

If Jack Simmons were asked which of the children he preferred most, he would without hesitation choose Jimmy, the second youngest of the brood. Jimmy was different. His curiosity was not generally of the criminal kind but was instead, delightful and sensitive. If he was naughty, it was more because he was a follower of the other children and therefore an accomplice by default. Heavens, it wasn't his fault that he was Maori. Yet, despite this natural mishap of birth, he had revealed a gentle and sympathetic mind which, Jack Simmons hoped, would help him transcend the natural leanings of his race in later life.

Unlike the other children, it had been difficult to get to know Jimmy. The others left you no choice for they intruded upon your life so much. You could say they forced themselves upon you. But even from the beginning, Jimmy had been the one who always hung back, who seemed to be waiting to be introduced. Jack Simmons liked that. He liked the solemnity in the boy, his tact and his courtesy. It was such a relief to discover that one of the children at least was equipped with manners! Mind you, all these good attributes could disappear when the six went on the rampage; but when you were alone with Jimmy, you were made aware of them through his demeanour and his diffident air.

Over the last three years, Jimmy hadn't changed for the worse at all. It would have been quite easy for his personality to be swayed or altered by his brothers and sisters. He still remained essentially the same child who used to ask:

'Mr Simmons, please, why are you cutting those branches off? Mr Simmons, does it hurt the trees when you cut them off? Is a macintosh *really* the same as a raincoat? Why is the same thing called two different names?'

Hopefully, Jimmy would grow up without acquiring too many of the Maori habits and characteristics displayed by the rest of the children. Jack Simmons held great expectations for him. The quicker Maoris adjusted to European life the better. It was no use their trying to live in their old careless manner. They had to have some regard for their neighbours, accustomed to a more private mode of living. An Englishman's home was his castle; he preferred it that way. And Jimmy would no doubt be found most acceptable as a visitor in any such home.

A pity you couldn't say the same of Tommy, the youngest of the six children. Four years old and already on his way to neighbourhood infamy!

Chuckling to himself, Jack Simmons walks towards the henhouse. On his way, he notices that Mark has left his bicycle leaning against the wall of the car shed. Or perhaps one of the Heremaia children has borrowed it today! His smile grows broader and he decides to put the bicycle in the shed where it belongs. He certainly has mellowed in the last three years! Previously, he would have become exceedingly angry if anyone, child or no, had borrowed something which belonged to him. Mind you, he still gets angry, but the sting of that anger has diminished now, only showing on the more unforgivable occasions. But one could not be angry for ever. There were other characteristics in the Heremaia family which redeemed them totally.

The greatest of these was their generosity. When the Simmonses had first settled in their new house they had had no furniture or cooking utensils because their household effects were still in transit from the landing port of Wellington. Sam and Millie had come to the rescue, and Millie had taken great delight in providing Maori bread along with the cutlery. Later, when the furniture arrived, Sam came around every day to help Jack Simmons move it into the house. He was a massive fellow and built like an ox. But like the children, he was also under Millie's strict thumb. It was always, 'Sam, do this' or 'Sam, do that' or 'Sam? Where the hell are you!' And it had been Millie apparently, who'd told Sam to get out the scythe and cut the Simmons' long grass when they were away on holiday one Christmas. When Jack Simmons thanked him, Sam had laughed and said he was only carrying out the boss's orders; then he'd quipped that the grass would come in handy for feeding his sheep. He had a small country run on which he fattened sheep for sale at the local livestock sales. Sam was a character. He was always bringing sweets home for his children. Millie used to get angry at him, but he told her that the sweets wouldn't do any harm as the children had rotten teeth already! He also brought sweets for Mark and Anne too. It wasn't fair if everybody's teeth weren't rotten, he explained.

All things considered, the relationship between the two families had been a very neighbourly one. Mark and Anne often went to the beach with the Heremaias. Sometimes, Sam would bring over a leg of mutton or a sack of potatoes. Once there'd been a hangi and Sally had thought the food delicious. The sight of kina had put her off, however, and she thought that puha was a little too rough for her taste.

Jack Simmons wheels the bicycle into the shed. He locks the door and then continues toward the henhouse. Raising hens is only a recent hobby of the Simmons family, and Jack Simmons is very proud of the results. His henhouse is only a small one and he doesn't have many hens, but Maria's eggs should be hatching out any day now. Poor Maria, she's suffered so much from the Heremaia children, always after her feathers.

Shaking his head, Jack Simmons reaches the henhouse. Strange, the latch isn't properly secured. But then he had been in a hurry this morning.

The hens cluck and gather at Jack Simmons' feet. They follow him to one corner of the coop where the grain bin is kept.

'All right!' Jack Simmons laughs. 'Don't be impatient now.'

He scoops grain from the bin and scatters it across the coop. The hens chase from one grain to the other. Jack Simmons watches them a moment. Then he goes into the henhouse where Maria is patiently sitting on her eggs.

'How are they coming, Maria?' Jack Simmons whispers. Maria clucks warningly at him.

'Let me see, old girl!' he continues. 'Let me see.'

Maria struggles as his hands close around her. He chuckles to himself.

'Don't be frightened, old girl.'

And slowly, the eggs are revealed.

There are eight of them. Two of them are still intact. The shells of the other six are cracked and the chickens can be seen within them. But the chickens have not hatched. They are dead.

Jack Simmons is stunned. If he was a child, he would weep. But because he is a man, he feels anger instead, deep and raging.

The latch not properly secured ... yet he definitely fastened it this morning. There seem to be scuff marks on the floor of the henhouse. Yes, here is the imprint of a small bare foot. The eggs *couldn't* have been broken by Maria.

Somebody has been here during the day. Somebody has broken these eggs. Obviously, that somebody was one of the Heremaia children. Only one of them would do such a thing.

Quivering, Jack Simmons puts Maria back in her nest. She settles herself upon the eggs.

'It's too late, old girl,' Jack Simmons whispers. 'But by Heaven, those children have really asked for it now.'

Jack Simmons stalks out of the henhouse.

'Sally? Sally!'

His wife appears at the doorway. She comes toward him.

'What's wrong Jack?' she asks.

'Those Heremaia children,' he seethes. 'They've really done it this time. I've told them time and time again to keep away from the henhouse. You've heard me tell them! I've warned them but, oh no, they keep coming and...'

'Jack! What's wrong!'

'What's *wrong?* Those kids are what's wrong!' he explodes. 'They've been in here while we've been away and...'

The sharp twanging of a wire screen door interrupts him. It is Henare. He waves to Jack and Sally Simmons, and comes running toward them.

'Hullo, Mr Simmons; hullo, Mrs Simmons! Did you have a good time today? Boy, we've missed you fellas.'

He grins and then begins climbing over the fence.

'Don't come any closer, boy!' Jack Simmons growls.

Henare looks up, alarmed at the tone of Mr Simmons' voice.

'Is there something wrong, Mr Simmons?'

He watches uncomprehendingly, as Jack Simmons walks to the fence and lifts his hand and...

'Jack!' Sally cries. She sees Henare slowly getting down from the fence and backing away, his body quivering. She sees his hands begin to cover his face and tears springing from his eyes. She sees the shocked look in the boy's face. And she hears her husband shout:

'And don't *any of you* set foot over this side of the fence again. You hear? You hear me?'

Sally turns to her husband.

'You shouldn't have done it, Jack.'

Suddenly, the Heremaia's back door twangs open again. Millie bursts into the backyard.

'What's up!' she shouts. 'What's happening! Hey!'

She runs towards her son and crouches beside him. The other children, attracted by the shouting, come to see what is happening.

'You kids stay in the house!' Millie shouts. Then she turns to Jack Simmons and her anger is dangerous.

'Boy, you better count yourself lucky that Sam isn't home,' she rages.

'Those kids have been into my hens again,' Jack Simmons thunders. 'They're a damned menace around here!'

'Which kids are you talking about?' Millie interrupts. 'Who are those kids you're talking about? Who are they?'

Her voice cracks out like a whip.

'Which kids? Who! Who!'

'You know which kids,' Jack Simmons answers.

Millie Heremaia laughs and it is glittering and sharp.

'Oh yes, I know whose kids. My kids, it's always my kids who've done it when something is wrong. Always my kids who are pinching your bike or breaking your windows. Nobody else's kids, oh, no. And it's always my kids who have been into your henhouse. That's what you think, eh! Well, I'll tell you something, Mr High and Mighty Simmons. They might have gone into your henhouse last time, but not *this* time Boy.'

'Come off it, Millie,' Jack Simmons yells. 'You know your kids as well as I do. You know they're a menace.'

'Don't you start telling me about my own kids!' Millie returns. 'Okay, so they're not perfect, but your own kids aren't perfect either. You go and ask that perfect son of yours what he was up to yesterday! You don't know do you? And I'll tell you why: it's because we Heremaias don't go broadcasting it around to every Tom, Dick and Harry like you do!'

'Now you hold on a minute, Millie.'

'It's the truth, isn't it? I know you, Jack Simmons! You're always talking about us behind our backs. Don't think I don't know. Your *Maori* neighbours, that's us, eh? Always pinching something; always lying. Well you listen to me and you better listen good. The Simmons family aren't the only ones who go off on a Sunday. Your Maori neighbours, they sometimes go out too. Yes, that's right, Mister. You get the message? Is it coming over loud and clear? Your Maori neighbours have been picking maize today. They only got back a little before you did. How do you like that, Mister Right? What do you think of that, eh?'

Millie Heremaia stands there, like a giant tree. Then she looks Jack straight in the eye and says the words:

'Why don't you go back to where you came from, Jack Simmons? You don't belong here, none of you. We never wanted you here in the first place.'

She puts her arms around Henare. Slowly, she guides him into the house. The door swings silently behind her.

Dinner that night is a strained affair at the Simmons house. The children are sent to bed early. Sally Simmons clears away the dishes and begins to wash them. Jack Simmons picks up the tea towel and begins drying them. After a while, he sighs.

'So I was wrong.'

'Yes, Jack. You shouldn't have done it.'

'But I haven't been wrong many times, have I Sally? You know those kids!'

'It doesn't matter about the other times, Jack. It matters about *this* time. And *this* time, you were wrong.'

'I couldn't help what I did, Sally. I got so angry, I just couldn't help it.'

Silence falls between them.

'Anyway,' Jack Simmons continues, 'Millie can't keep tabs on her children all the time. One of them could easily have sneaked out after they'd gotten home.'

'Oh, Jack,' Sally sighs.

'Well, blast it! Those kids were the obvious choice. You know what they're like: always up to something.'

'Not always.'

'Most times then! Just whose side are you on? You know what they're like; you know their reputation.'

'But Jack! Their reputation doesn't make them always the guilty ones. Can't you see that?'

Sally Simmons turns from her husband. She sits at the table, watching him. He bunches up the towel and throws it to the floor. Then he stares moodily out the kitchen window at the Heremaia house. Damn them, damn them.

'You'll have to do something,' Sally says.

'I know.'

'What are you going to do?'

'Apologise, I suppose. Go over there and apologise.'

'It would be best, Jack.'

'I feel such a blasted fool,' Jack Simmons whispers miserably.

'Everybody makes mistakes. You, the Heremaias, everybody.'

Silence falls again. Then Jack Simmons turns from the window.

'The sooner it's done the better I suppose,' he says.

He smiles at Sally.

'If I'm not back in ten minutes,' he continues, 'call the ambulance.'

He goes out and shuts the door behind him. Sally walks to the window and watches him. He waves to her and she waves back. Then she sees Jimmy at his window. Will Jimmy, will Annie, will any of the children ever come to see her again? And Henare ... what must he think of Jack now? Sally turns from the window. She decides to make a cup of tea for herself and for Jack. Poor Jack, he'll probably need it.

Could the children have done it though? Could they have gone into the henhouse? No. But you couldn't blame Jack for thinking that they had, could you? No, you couldn't. Still, he shouldn't have hit Henare. That was unforgivable. What a mess, what an awful mess.

Every conflict with the Heremaias has been a mess. Of suspicion, of doubt, of accusations proven or unproven. If only the Heremaias weren't so *large,* so obvious. They stick out like a sore thumb in the neighbourhood. They have not yet learnt the art of living with European people who may not understand their ways nor like them. They are essentially good people, but oh so tactless and troublesome at times. If only they would learn to be less obvious, and try to relinquish their obvious faults. Is it any wonder that when some accident happens in the street the Heremaia children are blamed? They bring it upon themselves, really they do!

Sally Simmons sighs helplessly. She puts the kettle on to boil. Heaven knows, she has tried to keep the crises to a minimum. She has tried to be a kind of Switzerland between her husband and the Heremaia children, an arbitrator between them. Sometimes she has been successful; other times, she has not. She knows that sometimes her husband's suspicions have been totally unfounded. This is one of those occasions, but there have been others. Jack couldn't seem to draw the line between judging the children on their reputation and on the facts of the matter. In doubtful issues, he just would not give the children the benefit of the doubt.

The goldfish affair had been one such doubtful case. Even now, Sally Simmons suspects, Jack still thinks that the Heremaia children were the culprits.

Then there was the time when she'd gone to the letter box and found one of the letters had been opened. Straight away, Jack had thought that the Heremaia children had been responsible. He was right too, for they had admitted opening the letter. They'd said it had been placed in their letter box and they'd opened it by mistake. The reason was plausible enough, but Jack hadn't believed the children. He did not trust them, and with good reason! If only they would stop telling stories. By doing so, they only sustained the mistrust.

For instance, when they'd been asked if they'd been inside the Simmons house when the family had been away for a weekend, they had first said No, then Yes, then No, then Yes again. It hadn't helped their explanation that they'd entered the house because they'd heard Silky, the Simmons' cat, mewing and they'd thought she was locked in. Their stories had already created mistrust of them. They could have been telling the truth, but then they could have been telling a lie. That was the trouble: after a while, you ceased to believe anything they said, whether it was the truth or not.

You couldn't trust the children. That was the main source of trouble. You judged them on their reputation. Most of all, you remembered that they were Maori. That was the most damaging evidence of all. Everybody knew what Maoris were like. You conveniently forgot the good points about the children. It wasn't your fault. They *helped* you to forget.

The kettle boils. Sally Simmons takes it off the stove. It had been wrong for Millie to say that Jack and she talked about her family behind their backs. Wrong and unfair. She and Jack had tried to understand the Heremaias. Not like some of the other neighbours who talked so grandly about 'our Maori people' one minute and then disowned them the next. And she at least tried to keep the bad behaviour of the Heremaia children in context. They were not always bad.

Sally Simmons looks out the window again. No sign of Jack. But there is Jimmy again. Poor Jimmy. Katarina had said he had the flu or something. Would he come to see her tomorrow? Lately he has been coming every morning to ask if the chickens have arrived. Only two of them will hatch now, Jimmy.

The curtain falls across Jimmy's window. And suddenly, Sally thinks: Could it have been Jimmy? No, it couldn't possibly have been him. It couldn't possibly have been any of the children! But then who could it have been? Who?

Thoughtfully, Sally Simmons prepares the tea. She hears the back door of the Heremaia house twang open. Jack is returning. Quickly, she gets two cups and saucers from the cupboard and begins to pour the tea. The door opens behind her. She turns and kisses her husband.

'Oh, Jack,' she sighs. 'I think it could have been Jimmy.'

'Jimmy?'

Sally Simmons nods. 'Who else could it have been?'

Her husband shakes his head. 'Perhaps it was the same person who stole the goldfish.'

'Oh no,' Sally says. 'Do you really think someone else is doing all this?'

'I just don't know what to think any more.'

Sally Simmons looks at her husband anxiously. She has always preferred to deal with certainties. The whole idea of someone else, someone unknown, being involved is too fearful to contemplate. After all, she and Jack had brought the children to New Zealand because it was, well, like home wasn't it?

'Oh Jack,' Sally says. 'The uncertainty...'

She changes the subject.

'It must have been terrible for you over there. What happened?'

Jack Simmons tells her.

He'd knocked on the door and Annie had answered. 'Go away, Mr Simmons,' she'd said. 'You're not our friend any more.' But he'd remained there and asked for Sam. Annie had said that he wasn't in. Then Millie had come to the door. 'Haven't you done enough for one day?' she'd asked. She'd almost slammed the door on him, but he'd prevented it from shutting. He'd told Millie he'd come to apologise. She'd answered that the harm had already been done.

'And then what happened?' Sally asks.

'Well, she finally let me in,' Jack Simmons answers. 'So there I was, standing there, trying to find the words to say. Millie didn't give me much of a chance. You know Millie! She really lambasted me. Her kids had been told not to go near the henhouse and they hadn't. They knew better than to disobey her. They weren't bad kids. Why was I always blaming them for things they hadn't done? She just went on and on and the children just kept looking at me. Just looking ... and then, as she was talking, Henare came into the passage behind her. Millie didn't see him. But I could see him. He just stood there for a moment. The light wasn't on in the passage. But it was on in the bedroom. And I saw his face, and the way he was looking at me and bunching his fists. It was a shock to see him like that, and I thought to myself, "Oh Jack Simmons, what have you done?"'

'It must have been awful,' Sally Simmons whispers.

'Yes it was,' Jack Simmons answers. His wife doesn't know the half of it. The names Millie called him, the terrible truthful things she said to him about his being a Pakeha.

Sally Simmons hugs her husband. 'Everything will be all right,' she says. 'If not tomorrow, then the day after that or the day following. You'll see.'

Jack Simmons tries to smile at her.

'For how long though, eh? Let's hope so. It's over now.'

He goes to the window and gazes across the fence at his neighbour's house.

Over?

And all of a sudden he sees Millie looking back across at him through the window of her kitchen. He realises that dealing with children is one thing. Dealing with adults is another.

You don't belong here, Jack Simmons, none of you.

Jack Simmons turns away. He and Millie will just have to work it out, whether they like it or not, want it or not.

On the other side of the fence, the lights go out in the Heremaias' house.

THE OTHER SIDE OF THE FENCE

By the time I came to the end of my year of writing, 1970, I had amassed quite a few Maori and (this might come as a surprise) Pakeha short stories. I put them into a collection – which I titled *Exercises for the Left Hand* because I'm a cack-hander – and schlepped them along to a number of publishers, without success. One of those publishers asked me, 'Who will read your book?' I said that Maori would. He answered, 'Maori don't read books.' I think I had earlier suspected that this perception of me personally and my work commercially might be a problem, so that's probably why the book was both Maori and Pakeha stories combined: have an Ace up your sleeve, just in case you have to play it and prove that actually you are a good writer, Maori or not.

Noel Hilliard came to my rescue. Jane and I were preparing to go overseas on a working holiday to the UK and Europe when Noel sent the stories to David Heap, then managing director of Heinemann Educational Publishers. Just before we left, in March 1971, David told me they would be interested in publishing a collection (I had told him I was also writing a novel, *Tangi,* and that interested him too), but he felt that I should concentrate on Maori stories. If I could assemble such a collection, particularly longer stories to go with the shorter ones, Heinemann would look at it; they would market it mainly to schools.

Well, at least I had half of a book, eh.

'The Other Side of the Fence' was one of the longer stories I wrote at David's suggestion. From my recollection, it was the first I wrote while Jane and I were living in our one-room bedsit just off Earls Court at 67 Harcourt Terrace, South Kensington. Jane would go off to work as a teacher at Hounslow East and, while I was able to score some jobs as an office temp, most of the time I sat at home writing more Maori stories ... and that novel. It was difficult to live in one reality and write in another. In this case, I was recalling the relationship between our family and the Waughs, a migrant English family who came to live next door at Haig Street. The relationship was quite tense to begin with, as two cultures with a fence between tried to come to grips with each other, and that was the symbolism that appealed to me: the story was about 1950s Maori and Pakeha relationships in a microcosm. I don't believe I was technically sufficiently equipped to write this story at the time I did; this story and 'The Whale' are the only ones in the book where I write from within someone else's head, and I didn't have the hang of it then. I had a second go with the revised *Pounamu Pounamu,* the 2003 edition, and it works better there.

In the end, Gordon and Jean Waugh became second parents to my sisters and me. We called them Mummy and Daddy Waugh. And their children, David, Janet and Annette, are our brother and sisters to this day.

Jean did indeed breed a beautiful goldfish of a mauve-rose colour. I can still remember the awe as my sisters and I watched it swimming; it was the most spellbinding sight I had ever seen.

THE SEARCH OF THE EMERALD CITY

We're leaving today!

'Kia tere, Matiu!' Dad shouts. 'We're going soon!'

Boy! This is exciting! E noho ra farm. E noho ra house. Goodbye. Hey! I forgot to say goodbye to Emere!

I jump down from the window and run out the door.

'Matiu!' Mum calls. 'Where you off to?'

'Just going to say goodbye to Emere, Mum!'

'E tama!' Mum sighs. 'Don't be long. And don't you dirty your clothes or I'll really give it to you!'

'All right, Mum!'

I climb over the gate and step carefully through the mud.

'Emere! Emere! Come to me, Emere!'

There she is! Down at the end of the paddock.

'Morena, Emere! No, don't come too close, you'll make me dirty. I'm going to miss you, Emere. You can't come with us. Cows don't live in the city. Guess what, Emere? We're going to make a lot of money! Dad, he says so. Emere, are you listening Emere? You just listen to me, you pirau thing!'

I swear at her, a bad word. And she moos and makes me feel sorry.

'I'm sorry, Emere, but you really are a dumb cow you know! E noho ra, friend.'

I give her a kiss.

'Eee, *Emere!* You need a wash!'

Then back to the house I run. First though, spit on my hands, wash my face, and smooth my neat clothes so Mum won't growl.

She gets crabby sometimes!

'Matiu!' Dad yells. 'Come and help me load the car.'

'I'm coming, Dad!'

'Aue!' he moans. 'That's a heavy box! What you got in it?'

'All my writing books, Dad. Miss Wright, she says I have to take them to my new school, that's what she says.'

'Can't we leave some behind?' Dad asks.

'No, Dad! I have to take all my books. Miss Wright, she says...'

'All right, all right. But what about this book?'

'You *can't* chuck that one away, Dad! That's my best. Neat story! About the straw man and the tin man and the cowardly lion and the emerald city and...'

'Boy, you can talk, Matiu!' Dad laughs. He hands me another box. 'Here, put this in the back too. Your Mum's stuff. What does she want to take all this stuff for!'

'Too much moan,' Mum yells. 'Turi turi to waho!'

She comes onto the verandah.

'Matiu! Where's that sister of yours? Where's that Roha gone?'

'Down the road, Mum. To see that Hone.'

My sister and Hone, they go around together. I know. I seen them kissing each other!

Hey! Look at our car! It's neat eh! Dad, he buys it from Mr Wallace. See? No dents. And honk honk goes the horn. And I can drive it, Dad said so. I'm a good driver!

Hey! Look at all those people coming! Coming to say haere ra. Tena koe Mr Parata, Mrs Parata. Tena koe Mrs Mohi. Tena koe, Nani Tama. Yes, Mum's in the house. No, you're not late, we're still here!

'Hey! Matiu!' someone calls. It's Hemi, my best mate! He waves to me to come and we run away from the house into the trees, and fall down laughing.

'Want a smoke?' Hemi asks. He lights one and puff puff puffs away.

'No, Mum might smell it. Where you been?'

'Down the river. And look what I got!'

He pulls out a hinaki head from his pockets, the biggest I ever seen!

'What a beauty, Hemi! Where'd you catch him?'

'Near the willows.'

I gasp. We been after that hinaki for a long time. They reckon he's so long, he has to go right out to sea just to turn around!

'I caught him for you,' Hemi says.

'Just for me?'

'Go on, take him,' he goes on. 'He's yours. Show those city people what a hinaki is. Go on.'

'Gee, thanks Hemi.'

We grow silent. We talk some more, but it's hard. Then Mum calls me.

'I have to go now,' I say. 'You coming?'

'No. Too many people.'

'Well ... e noho ra, taku hoa,' I whisper.

'Haere ra, Matiu,' he answers.

Then he is gone. My best friend. He'll always be my best friend. You just see!

'Where you been?' Mum growls. 'You have to help here! You better tell your father to lay off the beer. I'm not going to be driven by a drunk!'

'That's right, Hine,' Aunty Wiki says. 'You show your old man who's boss!'

The old ladies cackle to one another. Mrs Koko, who's hapu with her seventh, takes another swig at the beer bottle.

'Hey, Makareti!' someone yells. 'Lay off the brown bottle, eh! Your kid'll come out boozed!'

I run round the back. The men are drinking the pirau. Sonny is playing a guitar. Dad is speaking to Uncle Pita.

'Dad, when are we going?' I ask.

But he's too busy talking.

'Course I'm right!' he is saying. 'There's no jobs around here. Only the railways, the forestry, the Works, maybe shepherding.'

'Well brother,' Uncle says. 'I manage okay. Come back to shearing. You're still a gun at that game.'

'No, Pita. Me and Hine, we had enough of shearing. You shear for a few months and then what? Maybe some fruit picking or go down South to shear some more. No, I need a job all year round. Had enough of the gypsy life. The winters are getting too bloody cold! Wellington's the place. Plenty jobs, plenty money.'

'Boy!' Uncle says. 'Everybody's moving, the whole whanau.'

'Can't be helped,' Dad answers. 'I don't like to move. Waituhi is where our bones are. But we got to move. Not much room for pa living any more.'

'You're quitting too soon,' Uncle says. 'Can't you wait a while longer?

The koroua, Nani Tama, has another case before the courts on the return of our land. Things are bound to look up.'

'Must be the booze talking!' Dad laughs. 'No brother, we've been waiting long enough already. I've got to start looking to the future and to getting the kids educated. Boy, that's the story. My kids are going to get some brains. I want them to have better than I had. Easier than slaving your guts out. Me and Hine, we been working all our lives and we end up with nothing. You got to go where the money is. That's the Pakeha way.'

'The Pakeha way, the Pakeha way,' Uncle growls. 'And next thing you know, everybody is leaving.'

Dad looks at him sadly.

'Well brother, it happens. But you have to move with the times. And the times are not happening here in Waituhi. As long as I'm buried back here, that's all I want.'

Uncle cuffs Dad playfully.

'Easy on, brother! None of that talk! Still a lot of life left in you.'

'I don't know, Pita. Sometimes I feel my years. Feel old. Lost.'

'Hey! Come off it!' Uncle says. 'You better have another beer!'

I jump up.

'Mum says you're not to get drunk, Dad.'

Dad looks at me, a strange look.

'I'm doing it all for you, Matiu. All for you,' he whispers.

'Aw, Dad,' I answer. 'We'll make out. You'll see, you just wait and see.'

Mum comes round the back.

'E hoa, man!' she says to Dad. 'We better get a move on. Long way to Wellington.'

'Wait your hurry, woman!'

But Mum snatches the bottle from him.

'No more beer! I want to get to Wellington in one piece. Come on! We have to move.'

I follow Mum and Dad round to the front. The men follow too, suddenly quiet. The crowd gathers. Roha is with Hone, bawling her eyes out.

'Well,' Dad says after a while. 'I guess we'd better get on the road.' He turns to Nani Tama. 'Will you say a karaka for us, e pa?'

Nani Tama nods. Ever since his old house burnt down he is looking older and frail. But his voice is strong and although he doesn't want us to go his words are filled with love and beauty:

'Our whanau may be being dispersed to the far corners of the earth by the winds of change,' he begins, 'but none of you will ever be forgotten and you will never be lost to us. After all, you are seeds that were planted at Raiatea. Go forth on your unending journey.'

Then the prayer is over. Mum moves through the crowd saying goodbye.

'E noho ra, Queenie,' she says to Auntie. They press noses and the tears begin to fall. 'E noho ra, Nani. E noho ra, Hopa. E noho ra, Mum ... oh, Mum!'

Dad joins Mum, shaking hands, embracing, and doing the hongi. 'Farewell, taku hoa. E noho ra, my friends, my family. Taku Waituhi, e noho ra.'

These are my relatives, my whanau, my home. Now I am leaving them all and I am sad.

Sonny strums his guitar. All the people sing and sway softly. Mum has to get her handkerchief out.

E pari ra ngatai ki te akau
E hotu ra ko taku manawa. Aue...

The song draws to a close. There is silence and weeping. Mum stumbles into the car and hunches in the seat. Roha gets in the back. I get in too.

'E noho ra,' Dad whispers again. He starts the car.

The people wave as we depart. The car gathers speed. Mum sobs loudly. Dad is crying too. They look back.

The houses are getting smaller. We pass Rongopai. All the waving people become little flags fluttering far away. We turn onto the road. We leave Waituhi behind.

I look ahead. The road leads to Wellington, the big city. Emerald City!

Hey! I should be happy!

But I'm not, you know. I thought going away was supposed to be happy.

It is happy, isn't it?

I am happy, aren't I?

I look back.

We have been living in Waituhi all our lives, and that house disappearing was *our* house, and those people were *our* people, and we had green paddocks and Emere was our cow and...

E noho ra, Emere.

Stay away, tears.

THE SEARCH OF THE EMERALD CITY

At the time I was a boy, the great rural to urban migration of Maori was happening, from 1945 through to the 1970s. Maori were leaving their wa kainga for jobs in cities. Clearly, a people without a land base has no economic livelihood. Although my family, for instance, were now living in Gisborne, my father was still working as a member of the Smiler shearing gang, or sometimes for Robbie Cooper as shearer and labourer. The trouble was that the work was seasonal, so a lot of people had to be laid off during the winter.

Cities offered the prospect of more variety of work in factories, better pay and better education opportunities for children. I guess it was inevitable, therefore, that every year more families left Waituhi, mainly to live in Gisborne where the freezing works and Wattie's canning factory were. Some families migrated even further away, to Wellington or Auckland, and I could not help but notice that every year more and more houses in my beloved Waituhi were lying empty.

What set this particular story off was watching my grandmother, Teria, saying goodbye to one of her sons, either Uncle Mike or Uncle Win or maybe it was Uncle Mafeking. Sometimes a moment – in this case, my beautiful grandmother trying to be brave, not breaking down, and merely tracing the cheeks of her son with her fingers – is enough to create a huge sense of emotional loss, and I was witnessing such a moment. I wanted to capture that and, in particular, the eagerness of a young boy whose family is all packed up and ready to go.

I've used, in the title, imagery from Frank Baum's *The Wizard of Oz.* Later, I wrote other stories of that same boy in 'Yellow Brick Road', 'Return to Oz' and 'Kansas'. I like to think of this story – indeed, all the stories in *Pounamu Pounamu* – as my Songs of Innocence. In subsequent books, I expanded my work by writing my Songs of Experience, narratives of race relationships and the hugely difficult times for Maori as they traversed the Pakeha world and engaged with it, not only in urban areas but, ironically, also on their own turf.

ONE SUMMER MORNING

1

His room is a small one. Four walls, a large wardrobe inset with a full-length mirror, a little desk littered with his schoolbooks, a bookcase, a single bed spread with a quilt his mother has made, and a chair with a clock on it. The alarm is set for half past five in the morning. In four minutes it will ring.

The boy is still asleep. The blankets are drawn around his neck so that no air can get in to disturb the warmth. His head is burrowed beneath the pillow and there is just a small opening for him to breathe through. He sleeps covered like this because last night was very cold. Also because now that it is summer, the sun slants earlier through his bedroom window and would shine full on his face if it were uncovered. Then he would wake up before he needed to, and half past five is early enough to have to wake up as it is.

But the morning draws relentlessly on. The sun pierces through the foliage of the lemon tree outside the boy's window and makes the shadows of the branches and leaves leap and shiver and grow within the room. It lights up a pile of school clothes on the floor: cap, unpolished shoes, shorts, grey shirt and long socks. Then it pauses for a moment on the pencil marks on the wallpaper as if trying to rub them out. But they are indelible. A record, made by the boy, of how tall he has grown in the last five years. The topmost pencil line is very thick and almost cries out the boy's despair at not having grown at all in the last few months. Obstinately it registers and insists that he is still five foot two and a quarter inches tall. No more, no less. He can comb his hair higher if he wants to or put on his thickest soled shoes, but he will still be only five foot two and a quarter inches tall and he may as well get used to it. Anyway, that's tall enough for a thirteen-year-old boy isn't it? The sun moves away but pauses again at an opened exercise book. English composition: a story about pirates, in large writing so that the page has been filled with the minimum of effort and imagination. On the opposite page, the previous week's story has been commented on by the boy's teacher: 'Bears no relation to the subject set. No marks.' As if embarrassed, the sun moves away, across the bed where the boy huddles. The hands of the clock tick tock, and then the shrill bell rings to rupture the boy from his dreams.

'Go on then, you damn clock!' the boy thinks beneath the pillows. 'Ring until you're all rung out and see if I care. You're just fooling me, I know your tricks. Well I'm not budging. I'm not moving. It's not time yet. And anyway, it's too cold.'

The boy waits for the clock to stop but it grinds obstinately onward, a long incessant yell at him to wake up. He pretends not to hear, and finally the alarm begins to wind down, gives a few gurgles and bleats, and gives up. The boy is exultant, but then he hears three loud thumps on the wall and his father's voice grumbling and loud, calling to him.

'Hema! Hema, stop that clock.'

'It's off now, Dad!' the boy yells back, pulling the pillow away from his head. He listens, alert, as his father settles back to sleep again. Then he slides his head back under the pillow.

But the clock cries for vengeance. It seems to the boy that it is ticking and tocking more loudly: you must get up, you must get up, there is work to do, there is work to do.

The boy mutters to himself. But the clock has won as it always does and ticks with satisfaction at the sight of one small arm creeping out from beneath the blankets to grope for and finger the old clothes lying on the floor. The hand picks up a singlet and underpants and ferries them beneath the blankets. The bed arches and squeaks in tumult and then subsides. The hand appears again. This time, a shirt disappears. Trousers are the next to go, followed by a thick jersey and socks. Each time, mutterings and cursings issue in muffled despair from the bed, and minor earthquakes heave. Finally, the tumult subsides. For a moment, there is silence. And then a cautious foot slides slowly out of the bed, the toes twitch, testing the temperature, point down like a divining rod searching for water, delicately touch the floor, rebound with the shock, touch the floor again and resignedly teeter there like a ballerina's foot before lowering from toes to sole to heel. The other foot follows. And then the boy rises, still swathed by the blankets which now also cover his head, to sit there like a patchwork-quilted ghost.

Another day has begun. And like a beetle shuffling out of its protective cocoon, the blankets peel away and the boy appears.

With a groan, Hema lurches out of bed. He greets the morning with a yawn. Sleepily, he blunders down the passageway, thinking enviously of his two sisters who are still in bed.

'Why do I have to be the only boy in the family?' he grumbles to himself. 'Why does everybody pick on me! Georgina should have been a boy too. It just isn't fair!'

He passes his parents' bedroom and glares accusingly at the locked door. His thoughts are very rebellious this morning. Just as well his father cannot read them, otherwise Hema would get a clip over the ear. But the thoughts are soon gone. His mind becomes a piece of machinery, the tumblers clicking and turning, and prompting him to the chores he has to do every morning.

'First, light the stove,' his mind directs. 'What do you know! Georgina has actually done her job properly this time! The wood is all ready in the stove, but I bet you she's used green kindling again. And what's this? She's ripped up one of your comics for paper! How would she like it if you ripped up one of her stink love magazines? Never mind. Light the stove. You've read that comic anyway. No, don't use the kerosene to make the fire blaze, you know what your father said. No, don't do it. Well, don't blame me if he finds out. Now put the pots on to boil. One for the porridge and one for the tea. Good! Mum will be pleased with you this morning, eh.'

For a moment, Hema stands there, watching the wood burning. He turns his back to the stove so that his behind will get warm. But then the tumblers in his mind click again. Like an automaton, he obeys their orders.

Out onto the back porch he goes. His gumboots are waiting for him, cold and clammy. On they go! A quick wash at the basin in the bathroom. A bit of water here, a bit of water there, just enough to get the pikaro out of his eyes. Even that little wash makes him shiver. Quickly he grabs for the towel and rubs at his face, gasping and blowing and shivering, as if he'd just risen from the freezing Antarctic sea.

'We've got electricity but how come the water's always cold,' he moans. 'Our farm must be the only one in the world where the hot water is always cold. No hot water, no electric stove, no nothing! Jeez, this is supposed to be modern civilisation isn't it? And here I am, still having to chop wood all the damn time. It isn't fair.'

He grumbles bitterly to himself and thinks of his woes. A young boy like him, stuck out in the sticks while everybody else in the world must be having a good time in their flash city apartments and going on round-the-world cruises. And all those people, sipping at their champagne, they've probably never even heard of Waituhi. What a dump! But when he's a man, ah, watch out world!

He looks up and sees himself in the square mirror above the wash basin. For a moment, he is entranced. Then he turns his head so that his best side is showing and beams a slow and careful smile.

'Boy, you're handsome!' he whispers.

He winks. He makes his face stern. He cocks one eyebrow. Narrows his eyelids. Starts a slow, shy smile. Now a crooked one. Juts out his jaw. Turns to see his left profile. Aaargh! Another bloody pimple! Hastily turns to his best side again. Studies his hair just to make sure he hasn't got dandruff. Then smiles again.

'I'm a man, now,' he tells the mirror.

'Oh no you aren't,' the mirror replies in the voice of his mother.

'Oh yes I am!'

'Seeing is believing,' the mirror responds. 'I see it, but I don't believe it. You still look like a kid to me.'

'Don't you call me a kid! I'm thirteen years old.'

'But still a kid.'

'Just you look at this!' the boy yells. He thrusts his jaw at the mirror. 'Can't you see?'

'What?'

'My chin! Look at my chin!'

'Where?'

'The hair! Are you blind or something?'

'What hair? Look boy. You're only five foot two and a quarter inches tall and you better believe it. You're still a kid and you better believe that too.'

'So? I'm catching up to Dad anyway.'

'Yeah, but you aren't a man like he is.'

'I am so too! Just look at these muscles.'

'What muscles?'

'And look at this chest.'

'Sunken as it always has been. You're still a kid, just as you're still only five foot two and a quarter inches tall.'

'Aaah, shut your mouth!' the boy yells.

'And the same to you, doubled,' the mirror replies.

Hema turns away. A slow, triumphant smile spreads across his face. He turns back to the mirror.

'You think you're smart, don't you!' he leers. 'Well, I am a man and I got proof. You want to see it?'

'I know your proof, Hema,' the mirror sniffs. 'I don't wanna see it and you better believe it. You're too cocky, boy. Just because you're sproutin' hair all over the place, you're still a kid.'

'You're always pickin' on me!'

'I'm just telling you the truth for your own sake, boy. And while I'm at it, you're not so handsome as you think you are either. Your nose has got a bump in it and those lips! They're not lips; they're rubber tyres. You need a haircut. You got pimples and no amount of squeezing will get rid of them. And those teeth!'

But Hema has had enough. He walks away and goes down the steps to the wash-house where the milk bucket is kept. A firm grip round the cold handle and away he shuffles, head down, in the direction of the cow bail.

'Pick, pick, pick, everybody picks on me,' he mumbles to himself. 'They all tell me I'm still a kid, but I know I'm a man. Why can't everybody treat me like a man? Always pickin' on me.'

He mumbles all the way down the path, and the steam of his breath in the cold air is like smoke from a hard chuffing train. Still moaning, he comes within smelling distance of the outhouse toilet, suspends his angry thoughts and breath, hurries past, and almost disappears in steam as his thoughts and breath boil out again.

Clank, clank, clank goes the bucket as it swings against Hema's legs.

'Shut up, won't you!' he yells.

A fantail skips from a manuka and flits in cheekiness around him. He shoots it with his angry eyes.

And then, as he is approaching the gate from the house, he almost trips over a big clod of dirt.

'Why don't you look where you're going! Everybody picks on me.'

Everybody.

Even the latch on the gate is against him this morning. The frost has made it stiff and unwieldy.

'You bloody latch,' Hema swears. 'Move, you f.b. so and so. What the hell is wrong with you! You son of a bitch, you stinkin' f.c. of a b.b.!'

Suddenly, he lights on the right combination of words. The gate swings grandly open, and Hema stalks along the edge of the pine trees toward the cow bail. The ground is littered with pine needles and pine cones. Hema picks one up and throws it in the direction of the house. A loud explosion reverberates through the trees. Branches break, trees shatter and fall. Thoroughly satisfied, Hema turns again toward his destination. That'll show the so and sos! That'll teach them to pick on him!

He is in a better mood now and doesn't even kick the bucket with his fury when he discovers Queenie and Red aren't waiting for him at the cow bail. Mind you, they'll both suffer for this show of disregard for their lord and master. He'll pull their teats so hard they'll never forget it! They'll just have to be taught that he's not a boy any longer. He's a man and has been one for a whole two weeks now. Watch out, world! Hema Tipene is a man now! And why? Why has he become a man all of sudden? Because two weeks ago, two marvellous weeks ago, he, Hema Tipene, discovered *sex.*

2

'Tom, how do babies come?'

'Don't you know, Hema?'

'Course I do! I only wanted to know if you knew.'

'Don't tell lies! You don't know at all, Hema. Own up and tell the truth.'

'I know a little.'

'Hasn't your Dad told you, Hema?'

'A bit. I think he thinks I know already. I don't want to ask him because he'll think I'm dumb. But you're my cousin and you're eleven and I'm ten and I thought you should know and, well, I thought, I thought you could, you could...'

'So you're curious eh, cuz? Well, I'll tell you. You see, there's this stork and...'

'Don't make fun of me!'

'So you really want to know, Hema. Okay. A man and a woman sleep together and they make a baby.'

'Is that all?'

'Well not exactly. They do "it".'

'What's that?'

'"It"! You know. "It"! Jeez you're dumb! He uses his thing!'

'But that's rude! You're lying.'

'Well don't believe me then. Go and ask your Dad.'

'Dad wouldn't do that!'

'You wanna bet? That's how you got here. Haven't you ever heard of "it" before?'

'Course! But I never thought that babies came that way. That's rude.'

'No it isn't, cuz. It's sweet.'

'How do you know!'

'I've done it.'

'You teka.'

'All right then, don't believe me.'

'I won't.'

'All right then.'

'I still don't believe you.'

'Okay, okay.'

'I don't, you know.'

'Okay! Quit it! You make me sick.'

'I still don't believe you. Who did you do it with?'

'Somebody.'

'Somebody who?'

'Just somebody! I'm not going to tell you; you got a big mouth!'

'I won't tell. True I won't. Where did you do it?'

'In the bushes.'

'The bushes where?'

'Just in the bushes! Jeez, go to sleep won't you!'

'And you're sure that babies are made by doing it? You know, with your thing?'

'Aaargh, go to sleep.'

'I'd never have believed it. I don't believe it! But how does it work?'

'You really want to know, Hema?'

'Course I do. And you should know because you've done it.'

'There's nothing to it really! You just lie there and heave and snort and that's all.'

'That's all?'

'That's all.'

'But why doesn't the woman heave and snort all by herself then?'

'It's better when you both heave and snort together.'

'Oh.'

'It's fun, Hema.'

'It's still rude. Are you sure you did it properly?'

'I think so. It was fun, and Anita, she said it was fun.'

'You did it with that ugly thing!'

'She's not so ugly. Anyway it was dark so I pretended she was somebody else.'

'Eeee!'

'She called me her darling.'

'But tell me, what happens?'

'Hmmmnnn. Um, it just happens, that's all!'

'You don't know at all!'

'Course! It happens when you're about thirteen or older. Then you're a man.'

'What happens?'

'You become a man that's all! Jeez, I wish you'd stop asking these dumb questions.'

'But then, how come ... the baby?'

'The girl gets hapu, Hema. A big puku.'

'And the baby, where does it come out?'

'Haven't you seen cows having calves, Hema? The baby comes out like that!'

'True?'

'True. So now you know.'

'Yeah. Now I know. But are you sure?'

'I'm sure.'

'Are you sure you're sure?'

'Jeez, go to sleep won't you!'

'I still don't believe you did it with Anita.'

'Aaaaargh! Don't believe me then.'

'You didn't, did you!'

'Go to sleep!'

'I'm going to ask her tomorrow.'

'All right then, I didn't!'

'I knew! I knew you were a liar! I don't believe anything you've said.'

'Oh, for crying out loud.'

'But when did you say it happens, Tom? When you become a man? When you're about thirteen? Boy, I can't wait! But are you sure?'

'Go to sleep! Go to sleep! If you don't go to sleep, I'll give you a bloody hiding! Leave me alone. Please, Hema, leave me alone!'

'Okay. When I'm thirteen, right? Three years to go. What a long time to wait. What a long long long time.'

Looking back, Hema realises that three years wasn't so long to wait after all. In comparison the eight years to come before he is twenty-one seem a dismally long way off. Once, he used to look forward to the time he was thirteen. He is thirteen now and a man. But now he's got to wait until he's twenty-one, because then he'll be his own boss. It's not much good being a man when you're not your own boss. It just isn't fair! But who knows, eight years may sneak past him without his knowing it! Somebody might even invent a time machine and he'll be able to take a short cut to twenty-one. That would be just neat.

For the time being though, he decides to relish the idea of being thirteen and the tremendous thing which has happened to his body. For just two weeks ago, two fantastic weeks ago, his body coughed and wheezed and exploded into manhood and a little voice said in his mind:

'Well, Hema, you're not a kid any more.'

Mind you, the signs had crept up on him long before then. His shoulders started to broaden and his legs began to thicken out. Hairs began to appear in the most odd places, short and curly, and he used to look down at them and say:

'Shake it up, won't you!'

But the tiny tufts just sniffed back.

'Just wait your hurry, Hema Tipene!' they seemed to say.

However, Hema didn't want to wait. His friends' voices seemed to be breaking all over the place, but his was still like a squeaky kid's. So he took up sneaking smokes from his Dad's packet, because that was supposed to make your voice low and sexy. But then somebody told him that smoking stunted your growth so he gave it up. Oh, the agony of being only five foot two and a quarter inches tall! Everybody else was taller than he was and he was going to be a dwarf for the rest of his life. Worse still, he wouldn't be able to get a girl and what use would it be if he was a man then? He used to lie in bed and be haunted with dreams of himself sitting on the beach while all those beautiful girls wandered past him on their way to ogle a six-foot giant striking poses with his huge biceps and leopard-skin togs. And the next morning, he would rush to the wall and measure his height again.

'Five foot two and a quarter inches,' the wall would intone. 'No more, no less. And it's no use standing on your toes, Hema!'

It just wasn't fair. Why was he stuck with short parents? It was all their fault. Poor Hema, he would sulk all day.

'What's wrong with you now, son?' his father would ask.

And Hema would draw his breath, expel it, and blow his father to smithereens. After a while, he would calm down and a steely glint would appear in his eyes. Even if he was going to be short, he'd show those girls a thing or two. After all, being tall wasn't everything. You had to have powerhouse thighs, and he did, staying power which he definitely would have, and the last time he had measured his thing, it had almost driven him into fits of grateful hysteria.

And still the signs of his approaching manhood kept coming. Hundreds of people surely, had said to him:

'Pae kare, you've grown in the last few years! Is this really that little boy we knew before? Hey, you'll be busting out of your pants soon!'

Such remarks used to make him strut like a rooster and more determined to keep on wearing his tight school shorts to accentuate the obvious. He just loved hearing his relatives talk about him! He wasn't so keen though, if they said he looked like his father (Dad was ugly!) or like his mother (With her big nose? Not likely!), but he didn't mind when they said he was going to take after the Tipene side of the family. The Tipenes were renowned for being tall and also for their prolific breeding, legal or otherwise.

The trouble was, that only visitors to the family seemed to notice the changes in him. Homage wasn't at all forthcoming from his own family. There was the time when Uncle Frank had commented on Hema's fuzz and had said he better start shaving. All that day, Hema had gone around the house with his head cocked to one side, hoping that his father would see and take the hint. But Dad was as blind as a bat. And Georgina had said:

'Have you got a stiff neck, Hema?'

He could have throttled her on the spot. His big sister was always spoiling things. Nobody would ever marry her! She was going to be a spinster and a good job too.

His family was hopeless! All they wanted to do was keep him in short pants for the rest of his life. That had been another source of friction between himself and his father. He'd first asked his father to buy him longs when he was eleven. And here he was, thirteen years old now, and his knees were still exposed. What had Dad said?

'When you've got something to hide, Hema, then you can have long pants.'

What a dumb father. Couldn't he see? It just wasn't fair. All the other boys at school had long pants which they paraded around in at the pictures and dances. Yet he still had to sneak round in shorts. They made him look like a kid, even with the obvious! No wonder he hadn't had much success with the girls.

Hema sighs to himself. Nobody understands him, nobody sympathises with him. He'll just have to make a stand against his father. Have a showdown with him. Give me some long pants, Dad, or else! After all, he's a man now, and has been one for two whole weeks. Yes, he'll just have to make a stand.

'You and me have bin a long time together, Pardner, but this is where we go our separate ways,' he will say.

He levels a glance at his father, sitting on the other side of the card table in the Last Chance Saloon. The other drinkers scatter to the sides and the piano roll stops rolling. Somebody whispers, 'Get the sheriff!'

'Are you gonna give me those long pants?' he continues.

'Nope.'

'You're sure about that, Pardner?'

'Yup.'

The silence thickens. Blondie, the dancehall girl, screams:

'Don't do it, Kid!'

He cocks his eyebrow at her and aims a well-directed spit at the spittoon.

'Don't you worry about me, honey. Me and this here hombre have some unfinished business to attend to. Shall we mosey outside then, Pardner?'

'Yup.'

The street is dusty. The sidewalk empties of people. Out onto the street he and his Pardner go, spurs jingling while the sun shines at high noon. He turns and faces his Pardner. Regret shows on his face.

'You ain't changed your mind about them pants, Pardner?'

'Nope.'

'Then draw!'

His draw is lightning quick. Two guns spurt lead. He is hit in the shoulder. But it is his Pardner who falls. The smell of cordite drifts across the street. A woman screams, 'Murderer!' But he, the Kid, just blows at his revolver, spins it twice before slipping it in the holster, and then walks over to the still body.

'Why'd ya make me do it, Pardner? Why didn't ya just give me my pants?'

And he weeps there while a lone voice sings and violins play a Western song...

Yup. It'll have to be done, Hema decides. Man to man. A showdown with his father. Regrettable but necessary. For he, Hema Tipene, received the final proof of his manhood two weeks ago.

When it happened, it was a shock to Hema, but afterwards, he had been delighted. The dreams had started coming a little before that time, composed of one part actual knowledge and six parts imagination. Whatever he knew about sex from paperback books, toilet walls, discussions with friends and accidental sightings of girls down at the river made up the structure of the dreams. His imagination filled in the gaps, liberally and with an appalling disregard for the practicalities of the matter. When he awoke from these dreams he was stiff and sweating and he used to moan to himself:

'Hurry up won't you!'

Naturally, he wasn't addressing anyone in particular, but Dad used to think it great fun to yell from the other side of the wall:

'Who you talking to in there, Hema!'

Then Hema would hear his father and mother giggling and that put him in a rage. He'd pretend the sheet was his Dad and start boxing with it. Take that and take that you b.b. so and so, he would mutter. He'd kick with his legs and twist and turn, then start to panic because the sheet was strangling him. So he would give one mighty uppercut and dispatch his father forthwith. Trying to be funny, huh? That'll show him!

The waiting was the worst part. Sometimes he tried to will it to happen, but he gave that up quickly because he started to worry.

'Oh, gosh! What happens if I'm sterile?!'

The utter horror of such a thought. Doomed to a life as a eunuch. The living death. Or wandering through a world where everybody is having fun and he, poor lad, is unable to participate. Oh, misery!

At such times of stress, he, Hema Tipene, often performed an act which would have earned the scorn of his school friends had they seen him. He pulled down the blinds, knelt down, looked round just to make sure nobody could see him, made a house with his hands and...

'Our Father, which art in Heaven,' he would begin.

But even *He* seemed to be deaf, just like Dad. That was the trouble with older people: deaf, dumb, blind and mean! Think they own the world do they? Well, they better watch out for Hema Tipene!

And then all of a sudden, the long awaited event happened. On a Wednesday night (happy night!) it was, after the witching hour of midnight. He went to bed after having done his English and Maths and General Science homework in the usual five minutes, turned the lamp down and hadn't even given a thought to sex. Then the dream fell around him: a Bacchanalian delight obviously derived from a Roman epic movie he'd seen the weekend before. He, of course, was the dissolute emperor, munching on a bunch of grapes, his other six hands each around nubile slavewomen. A voice whispered in his ear. It was Claudia. She kissed his chest and the sweetness began. Softly. Unfolding. He the giver of sweetness and yet being given it. Participator and also spectator. Until with a shout, he brought the walls of Jericho tumbling down.

And he awoke, startled with joy, peered closely at the sheets for the final proof that his manhood had come at last. Jeez! Gosh!

He lay back in the bed and sighed. He was all right. He wasn't sterile. It had happened at last. And even though he was only five foot two and a quarter inches tall, he didn't care. Napoleon was short too! Tomorrow, he'd have to take a bath. What about the sheets? That's Mum's worry. Tonight, he was finally a man. Surprise, surprise, surprise.

His heart was thundering with relief and happiness. An owl hooted:

'Happy birthday!'

An opossum snarled its congratulations. The moon winked knowingly as it passed above a dark cloud. And it just felt so great to be alive and able! He sighed again and thought of the Claudia of his dreams.

'Oh, Claudia,' he whispered happily, 'peel me another grape.'

3

The morning sun shafts between the pine trees. Hema is standing beside the cow bail, shivering in the morning cold. His breath is hissing steam from his impatient nostrils. He has been waiting and waiting and still those blankety blank cows haven't come. And he has called and called and his echo has cracked the silence of the hills far away. He calls again.

'Queeeeeeennniieee. Rrrreeeeeddddd!'

Where are they! They should know by now that their lord and master demands their presence. Just wait till he gets them, just wait. He'll make them run all the way to the cow bail and they won't get any hay after he's finished milking them either. They'll be sorry!

Cursing to himself, Hema puts the milk bucket down and goes off in search of the disobedient cows. It is a dismal prospect because the paddock is a big one with two great humps in the middle and a steep incline to a patch of willow trees at one end. There are so many blind spots in the paddock too, and this means he'll have to go up into them to look for the cows. Gosh, his father was dumb putting a cow bail in this paddock. Just because *he* didn't have to do the milking every day. The pain of it!

Hema begins walking along the fenceline. Some of the battens are rotten and he kicks one to show his displeasure. Oh hell! It's fallen off! He picks it up and wedges it against the fence, otherwise Dad might get him to nail the whole fence up properly. It wasn't fair. It was always, Hema do this and Hema do that. Why wasn't Georgina a boy too? All she did was the cooking now and then and maybe washing the dishes. And even though he was two years younger than she was, he had to milk the cows, light the fire in the morning, feed the dogs and Mum's stupid fowls, chop the wood and millions of other things! But now that he's a man, aha, things are going to change around here. He'll soon crack that whip! And Georgina putting on all those airs as if she was a lady. Huh! She's as much a lady as her b. behind, and that's being charitable. He'll fix her.

'Georgina!'

'Yes, Master?'

'Get my kai, chop some wood, press my pants, comb my hair, make my bed, shine my shoes, cut my lunch, and then come here and kiss my ... You dogs just shut up!' he yells.

Hema has come to one corner of the seven-sided field and the dogs have started to howl and bark from the direction of the shearing shed. They rattle at their chains, hoping that Hema has brought them their breakfast. But he ain't no servant to dogs neither! The dogs begin to howl more loudly and Hema answers them. He lifts his throat into the morning air and...

'Oooowwwwwuuuuu,' he yodels.

The dogs rejoin in chorus, and for a few minutes boy and dogs embark on a cacophonic symphony of excruciating power. The melody screams through the air, is counter-pointed, floridly embellished with little barks and grunts and small squealed appoggiaturi from the pups, and then soars again. Then Hema laughs. He turns to the dogs and wiggles his behind. Stupid dogs! They'll just have to wait.

Everybody will have to wait now that he's a man! He sniffs disdainfully, delicately skirts two large cow pats, puts his nose in the air and his foot in a third.

'Aaargh!'

He retreats and a steely gleam issues from his diamond-hard eyes. Vengeance will be his, because he is the Lord. Just wait until he gets Queenie and Red. He'll teach them not to leave their deposits all over the place.

With renewed purpose, Hema continues to follow the fenceline as it zigs and zags back towards the house. He climbs the first incline and is gasping and chuffing for air when he finally reaches the top. He moans: does his father think he's a train? Fancy making this paddock the one for the cows! He looks to the front of him and looks to the back of him. He looks to all sides too. Queenie and Red are nowhere to be seen. Misery. That means they must be on the other side of the next hump, dang and blast it. He starts to walk in that direction when suddenly, he hears wild geese cackling overhead. He looks up and sees them, arrowing sharply through the bright cloudless morning. So beautiful they are, and they have all the sky as their dominion. Breathless with wonder and happiness, he watches them until they are like feathers falling over the pine trees and farmhouse, falling, falling, then gone. And with their going, he feels strangely sad. It is good to be a man, but how wonderful it has been to be just a kid! He looks down upon the farm and the house and caresses them with his memory.

To the left of him is the house. It is still and quiet and the smoke from the chimney is soft and grey. Is his mother up yet? From here, he can see the kitchen window.

And from here he can remember...

Our farm isn't flash, but we're lucky to have it. It's one of the 'pieces of broken biscuit' that were left to our tribe after most of our land was taken in the land wars. Dad's mother, Nani Miro, paid the rates on it until she died to make sure it stayed in the family. We still miss her.

The roof of our house needs painting again, but Dad will leave it as he always does for 'next year'. The guttering needs fixing too. There were bees in the roof last summer. Dad tried to get rid of them but almost burnt the house down. The bees are still there and will probably stay until the house falls down. It doesn't hurt when they sting. In the winter when it was cold, the bees liked to drop through the cracks in the ceiling and crawl into warm places such as the beds. Georgina didn't like that. But bees don't hurt when they sting. Old Bulla, the roadman, used to catch them with his hands, he wasn't afraid! They're only a nuisance in the summer when the grapes and the fruit trees are ripe. Last summer the grapes were purple-sweet and the bees soared all over the place in drunken delight.

Behind the house is the woodshed, the wash-house, Dad's tool shed and a few other sheds that aren't used. Mum has to wash the clothes by hand. Until Dad finally built the bathroom, all us kids were washed in the copper. In one of the unused sheds is a big stack of old newspapers and some of them have reports on the Second World War and

King George's England. One of the wild cats had her kittens in there, right on top of King George! That cat was just plain careless. She had a lot of kittens, but they went wild too. They would only come to Hine, my younger sister, and used to follow her as if she were their mother.

Next to the sheds is the vegetable garden. Mum got sick of waiting for Dad to build a fence around it so she did it herself. Before that, Bluey and Stupid, who are two of our horses, used to eat all Mum's cabbages. Stupid could eat anything! He used to come to the kitchen window and we would throw him the potato peelings and our kai if we didn't like it. The hens would come to the window too. And then we got Porky, our pig, and he used to join the hens and Stupid and snuffle around for the kai. Actually, Porky turned out to be a she and had some piglets.

The house is on a small rise, and beyond it is the garage for the truck, and the fowlhouse. We had ducks once too, but the dogs got at them, worrying them. Most of them died. Dad asked me if I'd like to rear some more, because the ducks belonged to me. I couldn't.

There were lots of fruit trees here, but most were chopped down by Dad when we moved onto the farm. The house was almost choked of light before. There are still lots of trees: lemon, orange, fig, plum, nectarine and even a loquat tree. The loquat tree bore fruit for the first time last summer. The trees all need pruning, but as usual, Dad says he'll do it 'next year'.

Beside the house, but a bit higher on the rise, is a huge outspreading walnut tree. Mum is afraid of that walnut tree, but she likes walnuts. Every winter, it creaks and sways and the wind tears the older branches away and flings them at the house. For a long time, Mum has been trying to get Dad to cut the tree down. Not 'Next year', but 'Now'! However, every time he says he will, then she changes her mind. If you cut it down, she says, it might fall on the house. Let it stand. First she's scared that it might fall down in the high wind, and then she's scared to have it chopped down. But then, perhaps she knows as I do about the opossum in that tree. He was there before we came, and he will probably stay there until the tree finally does fall down. We don't have guns in our house. Dad doesn't like shooting things.

In the front of the house and to one side, is the tennis court. We used to play tennis lots until we got tired of mowing the court. We only had a cranky push mower, and there were already enough lawns to mow. We're not rich.

Right in front is a big lawn. Mum used to grow flowers there until she finally decided that there were enough wild ones around to make the house beautiful. Everything grows wild now. The leaves from the trees fall in autumn. The grass grows wild beneath the trees. The flowers wither in winter. Fruit falls and remains to rot on the ground. And yet, everything is right somehow. The soil is nurtured by the fallen leaves and fruit, the grass tufts up to be eaten by the sheep and horses, and although the flowers die they come up again, the next year. There is some strange purpose here which does not need our help. We have beauty without cultivating it.

The lawn ends at a small stream which flows around the contours of the rise upon which the house stands. There is a footbridge over it and a path leading to the road where the mailbox stands.

Last summer, there were frogs in the stream.

To the right of the house, there is a small plantation which is always boggy because of the water from the stream. Where the ground is drier, a tall stand of pine trees grows. We used to drag sugar bags around with us and fill them with pine cones for the fire. One night, as we were watching from the back verandah, the moon came so low that it was suddenly caught by the leaves of two cabbage trees which were standing side by side, like two hands clasping at the moon. Georgina found a nest of baby stoats underneath the pine trees one day. We took them back to the house, but Dad made us return them before the mother stoat got wild with us. At the end of the pine tr
is the cow bail.

The shearing shed and yards are beyond the plantation. That's where all the hard work is done: the shearing, docking, dipping, pressing wool, machinery repairs, creosoting the battens, carpentry ... and the paint is blistering from the roof just as if it is sweating with the hard work too. There are four stands for the shearers and mostly Dad and his brothers shear our sheep. Dad's a gun shearer! He has the number one stand. When it is the shearing time, we saddle the horses and go out mustering the sheep. Sometimes Mum comes too on Gypsy. When Hine was a baby, Mum used to wrap her in a blanket and swing her over her back. It is hard work mustering. The sheep are dumb. The dogs are too, and chase the sheep all over the place except to where they're supposed to be shepherded. The biggest problem is getting the sheep across the river. The farm, you see, is divided in two by the river with the farmhouse and shearing shed on one side and the rest of the farm on the other. There is a narrow track joining the two parts and it descends steeply from the other side down to a swing bridge across the river, then rises steeply up to where the shearing shed is. Sometimes, when the sheep are really dumb, it takes a whole day to get them across the swing bridge. That's when Mum comes down and Georgina too, to lend a hand. It really makes you sweat! So sometimes we have a swim in the river to cool off. But that's not the end of it all, oh no. The sheep have to be put through the race at the yards next to the shearing shed. That's where the ewes and hoggets and lambs are separated for the shearing. Then when the shearers come, Dad starts the old engine in the shed; it coughs into life and provides the power for the shearers' handpieces. Shearing the sheep takes a long time. Mum, Georgina, my uncles' wives and my girl cousins do all the fleeco work and sweep the board. I am the sheepo, and sometimes Hine helps me. My bigger boy cousins do the pressing because I'm not strong enough. Soon I will be! It is a good life.

When the shearing is finished and everybody leaves, it makes you feel a bit lonely. Not for long though, because there's still a lot to do! The sheep have to be taken back across the river and the odds and ends tied up at the shed. Later the big trucks come to take away the bales of wool.

Sometimes, for a holiday, the whole family goes out scrub cutting. There is a lot of scrub on our farm and we use hooks and axes to cut it down. We stay in a small hut on the other side of the river. In the morning, Mum cooks breakfast, then we all hop on our horses and go to attack the scrub. Mum, Dad, Georgina and I cut the scrub. Hine piles it in heaps. Then Dad sets fire to it and the smoke billows thickly across the hills. At smoko time, Mum puts the billy on. It's a lot of fun.

In the docking season, it is fun too. The tails of the lambs have to be cut off or else they get dags. When we were young, us kids used to trail behind Dad and as soon as the tails dropped off the lambs, we would grab them and grill them over an open fire, then scrape away the burnt wool and eat the tails. Neat, boy!

And always at night time, we would come to the farmhouse. It is very big for our small family. There are four bedrooms, a huge kitchen, a pantry, and a long sitting room with a big open fire. In winter, Mum and Dad bring their bed into the sitting room and sleep beside the fire. We have a lot of books including a whole set of encyclopaedias that a salesman sold us. We have Chinese Checkers too. No television though. But we're so busy, I suppose we wouldn't have time to look at television anyway. In winter, it is good to play in the sitting room while Mum and Dad are in bed. You can watch the fire leaping in the grate if you're bored. The fire leaps and curls and crackles and sometimes it sizzles when the rain falls down the chimney.

Then, when Mum and Dad are tired and want a moe, they send us to bed. So we each take a lamp to our rooms and they make beautiful golden patterns on the wallpaper.

This place is where I, Hema Tipene, have lived all my years as a kid. It has been a happy time. Now that I am a man, I am sorry to leave those times behind.

He sighs, this boy, as he looks down upon the farm.

If it has to be, he thinks, it just has to be! Who knows? I might have better times now that I'm a man. Watch out, world!

Hema turns to look for the cows again, but suddenly he hears the back door of the house slamming shut. He looks down and an impish gleam lights his eyes. He sees a figure, her hair still in curlers, putting on her gumboots and shuffling down to the outhouse and shivering beneath her brunch coat. It is Georgina, the queen of the house, off to sit on her throne. And from where he is standing, Hema can see right inside! He chuckles to himself. He'll fix her! Jeez, she looks ugly. If only her boyfriends could see her now. He waits and watches. Georgina opens the door, bends down to inspect the throne, then turns around, gives her behind a few wiggles, arranges herself comfortably on the seat, sighs and stares uninterestedly around her. As usual, she does not close the door, just sits there in all her radiant beauty. And

Hema cups his hands to his mouth and calls:

'I can seeeeeeee yoooouuuuu!'

And Georgina's shriek of fright rends the air.

'Who's there! Who's watching! Go away!'

She starts to call for her father. Then she sees Hema dancing and doubled up with laughter. He is thinking: perhaps she wet her pants!

'Just wait till I get you, Hema Tipene!' Georgina screams. 'Just wait! I'm going to tell Dad that you're spying on me!'

She lifts herself up carefully and grabs at the door to pull it closed. Her voice still booms out from behind it.

'Don't think you can get away with it either, you little bugger! I'll get you when you get back! I'm going to tell Mum and Dad too, and Dad will give you a good hiding, you little shit.'

But Hema is too busy chortling to himself to listen. Serves her right. That'll teach her! Ana!

In a much better mood now, he walks down the incline, pants up the second hump and spies Queenie and

Red. They are sitting under the willow trees, right up in the highest part of the paddock. Furious again, Hema steams down the hump and stands at the bottom. He points his finger at the ground, looks up at the cows and disappears in fire and brimstone.

'You fellas just come down here right this minute! Queenie?! Red?! You hear me up there? If you think I'm coming all the way up there, you better think again. Now hurry up, I haven't got all day! Didn't you hear me you effing-blasted-bloody so-and-so cows?! Come down here this minute! Queenie! Red!'

'Mooooooo,' Queenie says.

Red just sniffs, licks at her nostrils and continues chewing her cud. Whoever is that little boy down there hopping around?

'Pae kare, you fellas!' Hema yells. 'See this stick? Well I'm coming up there and I'm going to lay into both of you. Just you wait. Just you wait!'

Swearing to himself, Hema pulls at the grass and climbs up one side of the steep hill. Everybody is picking on him today. Everything is against him. It just isn't fair! And those cows, they'll soon see who's the boss! He'll slap their haunches and tie their tails in knots and they'll be sorry. He finally gets to the top, opens his mouth to scream at the cows...

But they are gone. He looks around and is just in time to see two brown behinds swaying saucily over the first hump.

Misery. Oh gosh, all this way for nothing. Why was he ever born?

Utterly dejected now, Hema wanders back after the cows. Down the hill, up the hump and down the hump, up the rise and down the rise, and along the line of pines to the cow bail where Queenie and Red are waiting. He stares at them for a moment with a hurt expression in his eyes. And they stare back with their wide innocent eyes.

'You fellas are mean to me,' Hema tells them.

'We're not going to be yelled and screamed at,' the cows seem to say.

'I didn't mean all those things,' Hema sniffs. 'I wouldn't hurt you fellas. Tomorrow, you be good and be here waiting for me, eh?'

The cows lower their heads. Hema pats Queenie first, and she sways into the cow bail, while Red wanders off to chew the time away before it is her turn. In the bail, Hema sits on the stool, greases Queenie's udder, puts the bucket between his knees, snuggles his head into Queenie's belly, and begins to pull gently on her teats. The back two first. Then the front two afterward. The milk spurts rapidly into the bucket, warm and frothy. And as Hema milks the cow, he talks to her. His eyes glaze over, his dejection falls away and he sighs:

'Oh, Queenie! I'm a man now.'

4

'Hey boys! I've got a juicy book here!'

'Where!'

It is lunchtime at school and Hema has joined some of his mates under a tree where they are shaded from the sun. Fats Matenga has wobbled over, bearing a paperback in his quivering hands.

'Giz a look, Fats.'

'Hold your horses, boys! Hey, lay off, Jackie, it's my book.'

'Cut the noise, Fats! One of the teachers might hear you. Jeez you make a noise and a half. Where are the good bits!'

'Good one on page ... ah, here we are! Gather around me, boys, and listen to this!'

...James Able stopped at the door. He put his hand on the doorknob and suddenly, he froze. Someone had been here. He could tell, because his Secret Agent eyes had discerned faint fingerprints on the polished brass. As quick as a flash he dropped on his knees and withdrew his Smith and Wesson from his shoulder holster. He listened, his well-oiled body keen for action. Somebody was in the room! Who could it be? Maybe it was the Spider, mastermind of the Alpha Operation which he'd come to investigate. His body tensed. His handsome face became cruel and savage. He patted at his hair, wrenched the door open and threw himself in.

'Oh James!' *a voice cried.*

It was beautiful blonde Natasha, standing next to the big double bed. James Able ran his eyes over her long, sleek body. She was wearing a see-through negligee, and what he saw, he liked. Underneath, she was naked...

'Jeez!'

'Don't stop, Fats! Hurry up!'

'Okay, okay!'

...James Able walked purposefully over to the girl, cowering and panting to herself. He gripped her by the shoulders and she screamed.

'What are you doing here, Natasha?' he asked dangerously.

'You're hurting me, James!' she answered, biting her beautiful and luscious lips.

'Tell me!' James Able insisted.

Natasha leant against him and he could feel her warm ripe body against his. She was wearing 'Dangerous Desire' perfume.

'The Spider sent me here to kill you,' Natasha sobbed. 'I'm a Russian spy.'

James Able recoiled with horror. 'Not you, Natasha! I trusted you!'

'Yes, James!' Natasha wept. 'But I couldn't do it. You see, I love you. Oh, James, James, James, James...' she whispered over and over again.

'You know what this means?' James Able whispered.

'Yes, James,' Natasha nodded. 'You must kill me.' And she ripped off her negligee. 'Kill me quick!'

She stood there, naked.

The sight of her blinding beauty made James Able sick...

'Hang on, boys. I have to turn the page.'

...of his mission.

'I can't do it, Natasha,' he said. He stepped up to her, looked down into her violet eyes, and kissed her brutally on the mouth. She went limp against him.

'Oh, James, James, James, James', she whispered over and over again. 'You're hurting me, James! It's so big! I can feel it protruding.'

James Able threw away his Smith and Wesson.

'That's better,' Natasha the Russian spy sighed. She pressed his head against her breasts and moaned as he

kissed them. Then James Able picked her up in his muscled arms and carried her over to the big double bed. He was raging with desire. Natasha reached up and began unbuttoning his tailor-made shirt. He shuddered as her cold hands caressed his manly chest. Her fingers came lower and lower and began unbuttoning his trousers...

'Jeez.'

'Don't stop, Fats!'

...and he felt her well-manicured fingers caressing his thighs.

'Oh, James,' Natasha whispered. 'Why do you need a gun?'

'Quick, turn the page!'

...The next day, James Able awoke and Natasha was gone. He got up, showered, put his shoulder holster on and...

'Hang on, Fats. What happened in between?'

'Yeah! What happened?'

'That's all, boys.'

'That's all? You mean there's no more? Scrag him!'

'Hold on, boys! Hold on! Jeez, can't you fellas use a bit of imagination!'

'Aah, let him go, fellas,' Jackie Smith says. He gives Fats a shove to send him on his way. 'These Intermediate kids!' Jackie laughs.

'Yeah.'

The group laugh with one another. Then Jackie, the big man of the school, signs for attention.

'Listen boys. Here's a story for you, and this is for real. Me and Sam here were down at the river last weekend.'

'Yeah, that's right! We were too, and we saw...'

'Who's telling this story, Sam? You or me!'

'Sorry, Jackie.'

And the story begins, with the boys sitting rapt, beneath the willow trees at school.

At thirteen, Hema Tipene knows all there is to know about sex. He has been well grounded in the theory of the matter and is looking forward to the time when he can put his fantastic knowledge into practice. His thoughts are healthy even if they are slightly colourful, and are certainly not dirty. Sex is so much a part of adult life, and now that he is a man, it seems only natural to know all there is on the subject. It must be important, mustn't it? Why else would girls and boys go through puberty! There must be some purpose to that great rupture in a boy's life. What use is it, if you don't take advantage of the possibilities it grants you. With such a gift, you could rule the world.

And so Hema waits, with brimming excitement. He'd be the last to say he had a one-track mind, and it wouldn't be 'dirt track' either. No, he is just curious. After having lived thirteen years ignorant of sex, he has finally discovered it. His expectations are a little too hopeful, poor boy. Like his heroes of fiction, he expects to smile at his heroine on page three and bed her on page four. He disdains the idea that it can be more difficult than that. He has a lot to learn about the whole absurd business of courtship and the crafty wiles of women. The next few years will burn him to a frazzle and he will emerge from his campaigns utterly exhausted and empty-handed. At the moment, however, he feels very optimistic. Even if he is only five foot two and a quarter inches tall, he is handsome (in his own estimation), sexy and best of all, available. He's not getting married in a hurry! And there must be thousands of girls just waiting to get at him!

'Isn't he gorgeous?'

'Oh, he's so handsome!'

'I must make him mine.'

'Oh, those sexy legs. Those eyes. Those lovely rubber lips. Mmmmm. Those feet, those toenails, those muscles, those hips. Mmmm, do what you wish with us, Lord!'

Hema gives a delicious sigh. It's all going to be so very, very easy. And he will stride manfully past those entreating figures, pointing his finger at each one and mumbling:

'Eeny, meeny, miney, mo.'

Yes, girls have suddenly become important in his life. Previously, he has been utterly uninterested in them. At first, as far as he was concerned, the difference between himself and girls was that he had one and girls didn't. As he grew, however, he noticed other subtle differences. Girls had long hair, they wore dresses, they played with dolls, they couldn't climb trees, they were cissy, they cried a lot. And worst of all, boys weren't allowed to hit girls, but girls could hit boys if they wanted to. That just wasn't fair!

But the really important difference hadn't hit home to him until he was told he had to take a bath separately from his sisters.

'Why, Dad!'

'Because you're getting to be a big boy now and Georgina is a big girl.'

'But we've always had a bath together before!'

'Well things are different now.'

'How different?'

'Lord preserve me. Georgina is growing up, and she's getting shy. She just doesn't want to have a bath with you any more. Anyway Hema, you're always complaining about Georgina taking all the room in the bath, so what's your worry?'

Thereafter, the differences between boys and girls seemed to multiply until he finally took them as a matter of course without really understanding why. But one other thing he discovered in those early years was that women had babies and men didn't. That was very puzzling. He also discovered what his thing-that-girls-didn't-have was for. Not only for having a mimi, true! But he wasn't the least interested in its other function. He was too busy playing with his trucks. He never batted an eyelid when he saw animals together in the paddocks, he cast an uninterested eye over his sister without realising she was growing a bosom, and was utterly bored at his father's apoplectic efforts to explain about sex. Oh, he was such a dumb kid! But now, aha, things have changed. He's not that same stupid kid any more.

For instance, this isn't the same kid who guffawed at the sight of his uncles swimming nude in the river. He will no longer creep up on kissing couples in the movies and screech: Eeeeeee! Nor will he think girls weren't good for anything. That kid's name couldn't have been Hema Tipene. Hema Tipene was born only two weeks ago! Girls are marvellous, girls are fantastic but luckily, they're not out of this world! Not for Hema Tipene the secretive making love with his hands. Nor for him, the oglings of cissy Dick Simons. And if any bloody kid ever creeps up on him and a girl in the pictures, he'll give that kid what-for!

Yes, Hema Tipene is ready to straddle the world. In preparation for this big step, he has begun to mould his personality and character to fit the required earth-shattering image. The kid who once used to be careless about his appearance will soon spend a half an hour combing his hair. Not any longer the 'once through the hair and that's it' trick. Oh, no, this lad will comb every strand into place, worry whether it is windy outside, and regard any fall of dandruff as a certain sign that he is going bald. If he is tackled in a rugby game, the first thing he will do is whip out his comb and too bad if the other side scores a try. He won't wash his face only once a day, but as often as he can to rid his complexion of excessive oiliness. He will read that it is oily skin which causes pimples and an imminent pimple will be, for him, a terrible disaster. His clothes will have to be pressed every day and even then, he will walk like a wooden soldier so that the pants don't get creased. He will inspect his face every day, sometimes marvelling at the profile and then moaning because of his big nose. He will be sometimes confident, but the slightest suspicion of not being able to measure up will make him miserable.

This boy will also become 'one of the crowd'. It will be a great relief because it will mean he is socially acceptable. Like the crowd, he will shuffle around with his hands in his pockets. He once used to run, but from now on everything will be done slowly: that way, it looks sexy. He already wears his cap at a rakish angle and his school socks round his ankles. When addressed, he grunts. Maybe he smiles, but only for a while, as it might crack the carefully cultivated sneer on his face. He is always seen with the boys and one of their favourite topics is girls. But would he ever talk with a girl? Never! Oh no, for the sad truth is that this boy quails at the impending approach of any girl. Excluding his sisters, who don't count. But he does not shuffle and grunt in vain. All this is practice, and is designed to impress the girls. It is his 'public image' emerging. But away from the public eye an astounding change takes place, and he becomes Hema Tipene, the hick-town Hori, again. For the next few years, his personality and appearance will change time and time again like a barometer gone wrong. In the end, he may strike a happy medium of carefully cultivated carelessness. Better still, he just might see the light and decide the effort just isn't worth it. For the time being, he plays it by ear. He is half-man, half-kid and some days he is all one or all the other. Misery!

But another beginning has been made in Hema Tipene's life during the last two weeks. Not only has he discovered sex and girls, but he has also fallen in love with one of the species. He regards this phenomenon with great relief for it should lead soon to his next discovery. Hema Tipene is thirteen years old and has never been kissed! The girl's name is Claudia Petrie, called 'Claude' for short because she is such a tomboy. In Hema Tipene's opinion, they were made for each other. Ah, Claudia.

To be fair, Claudia Petrie is not ugly. In fact, she has rather a charming smile. Hema sees great potential in her development. She is the next step onward from his previous infatuation with toy trucks. Claudia is the daughter of one of the teachers at Hema's school. She loves riding horses, a passion which is decidedly in her favour as far as Hema is concerned. It doesn't really matter that she is three inches taller than he is; he's not going to be five foot two and a quarter inches tall all his life! And anyway, she is the only girl so far to take any interest at all in him. At the last school dance, she actually strode over to him and asked him for a waltz. How his heart thundered then! He held her at arm's length, gritted his teeth and whispered to himself: one two three, one two three. And he was sure that everybody was watching! Mum and Dad had seen him, and Dad had nudged Mum. Hema's face had grown longer and more embarrassed. But Dad hadn't laughed. No, he'd kept his face straight all the time and it had only been Mum who'd giggled. Oh, they were proud of him!

After the waltz, Dad had even come over and given Hema some money to 'buy a soft drink for your Pakeha girlfriend'.

Before that dance, Claudia Petrie had just been another girl. After it, she was the one and only. And Hema would watch her playing basketball during lunchtime and be in absolute agony.

'Claudia, I love you.'

He would never ever think to tell her of his love. For the time being, he loved her from afar, because she, apparently, had forgotten all about that tumultuous waltz. Her flippant 'Gidday, Hema!' whenever she saw him was both sheer ecstasy and sheer pain. Couldn't she see how he was being tormented? Oh, the pain of loving and not being loved in return! Often, as Hema was watching her, he would think:

'When her friends have gone away, I'll go up to her. I'll say: "Claudia." And she'll whisper: "Yes, Hema?" And then I'll ask her: "How'd you like to come to the pictures with me next week?" And she'll look up at me with tears in her eyes and say: "Oh, Hema." And then she'll give a little nod of her beautiful head and maybe our hands will brush and if they do, I'll take her hand and hold it and then we'll belong to each other. And then I'll wait for Saturday to come and I'll say to Dad: "Dad! I need some money!" And he'll ask: "What for?" And I'll say: "Because I'm taking Claudia Petrie to the pictures." And he'll say: "Oh, that lovely girl you were dancing with?" And I'll say: "Yes, Dad. That's the one." And then, because I haven't got a licence, I'll ask Dad: "Will you drive me down to the pictures?" And he'll say: "Of course!" Because Dad himself thinks that Claudia Petrie is the best looking girl in town. So I'll get dressed and maybe by Saturday I'll have some long pants, and then Dad will drive me into town and drop me off outside the picture theatre, and Claudia will be there and she'll be so beautiful. And I'll take her hand and whisper: "Hullo." And she'll whisper back and hold my hand. And I'll ask her: "Do you mind if we sit in the cheap seats because then we'll have enough money to buy icecreams at interval!?" And she'll say: "Anything you say, Hema, darling."'

And so Hema would continue to dream. But by the time he finally worked up enough courage to ask Claudia, she would have gone. Misery.

In the last few weeks, Claudia Petrie had driven Hema to the depths of despair. What's the use of being a man if you haven't got a girlfriend? His mother and father aren't much help either.

'What's wrong with you, Hema! You're always mooning around the place. If you haven't got anything better to do, go and chop some wood.'

Why can't parents understand? Here he is, Hema Tipene, just wasting away and all they can think of is getting him to chop wood. It just isn't fair! Life is harsh. Life is one long longing after a skinny, tall Pakeha girl called Claudia Petrie.

In his more desperate moments, Hema would go into the bathroom and look at himself in the mirror. And there, amid the toothpaste and bath soap and scrubbing brush, he would whisper: She loves me, she loves me not, she loves me, she loves me not.

'Oh say that she loves me!' he would entreat the mirror.

'Don't be stupid!' the mirror would intone.

'But she must, she must.'

'Why must she? You ain't no raving beauty.'

'Neither is she, but I still love her.'

'She's better than nothing, but what do you know about love? You're only a kid!'

'I am not either. I'm a man.'

'You listen to me, Big Ears. You're only a kid still and you better believe it. Anyway, that Claudia Petrie wouldn't take a second glance at you.'

'Why not?'

''Cause she's taller than you, and Pakeha too. And you, you're as black as they come and only five foot two and a quarter inches tall.'

'Can't you think of anything better to say? Why are you always pickin' on me! I'm going to crack you one day!'

'Boy, you better not! If you do, I'll give you seven years of no girls and that won't do your manhood no good!'

'Wrap up and go bite yourself.'

'And the same to you doubled,' the mirror would sniff.

Poor Hema! Nobody likes him, everybody picks on him and the only girl in the world doesn't love him. But wait, is that she, calling from afar? Oh, how beautiful she is, running in slow motion with a Hollywood orchestra playing behind her!

'Heeemmmaaa!' she calls. She lifts her hand to wave slowly to him. Along the fenceline toward the cow bail she comes, oblivious of the cow pats. Her hair streams behind her, her hat blows free from her hair and is gone with the wind. And he, Hema Tipene, rises from his seat and lifts his arms to receive her. Onward and onward she comes, her long gingham dress flowing and curling softly around her skinny legs. The orchestra thunders, the clouds go by, red sails in the sunset, and suddenly she is there, swooning in his arms. She palpitates against him and there are joyous tears in her eyes. He pulls her to his manly chest. And she lifts her head to receive his lips.

'Kiss me as you never have before,' she cries.

And he does as she commands.

Right smack bang on the bristled behind of Queenie who kicks him back into the sad, sad world of reality.

It just isn't fair!

5

A voice calls from far away:

'Hema! Hurry up with the milking, we can't wait all day!'

It is Mum and she is her usual grumpy self this morning. Hema pokes his tongue in the direction of her call. It elongates, sidles through the trees, over the gate and along the path to flap rudely at her. Nobody's going to shout at him any more!

'It's all your fault,' Hema says to Red. 'You and Queenie are mean to me and just look at this mess!' He points to the large pool of milk, spilt from the bucket by Queenie when she kicked him. What will Mum say? There's not much milk left in the bucket because Red has refused to give. Oh well, he'll top it up with water and Mum won't know the difference.

Hema finishes milking, stands clear and allows Red to sway out of the cow bail. Gosh, he is very late this morning. Worried, he picks up the bucket and hurries back to the house. But before he goes, he casts a murderous glance at the two cows.

'You fellas better be waiting for me tomorrow,' he warns, 'or else! You hear me? You hear me you dumb cows?'

Then, muttering to himself, he walks quickly along the pine trees, through the gate, and forgets to breathe deep before passing the outhouse. The smell is foul and he staggers as if asphyxiated. Oh, when are they going to have modern plumbing around here!

'Hema!' his mother calls again from the depths of the kitchen.

'I'm coming, I'm coming!' he screams. He takes the milk into the wash-house, strains it into a large can, looks furtively around before running cold water into it, and then carries the can onto the back verandah. Off with his gumboots, and another quick wash before opening the door and placing the can on the floor.

'Got you!' someone screams behind him. It is Georgina, and she is livid with anger.

'Lemme go, lemme go!'

'Dad! Da-aad!' Georgina yells. 'Here he is, here he is!'

'Lemme go, Gina!'

Georgina bares her teeth and whispers to him:

'I'll teach you to spy on me when I'm in the lav, you little shit!'

Then she calls again to her father.

'What's up! What's happening here?' Dad moans.

'Dad, Hema was spying on me!'

'She swore at me, Dad!'

'Stop trying to wriggle out of it. You were watching me. Dad! I want you to give him a good thrashing.'

'Dad, she swore at me. She called me a little ess-aitch-eyetee!'

'I did not!'

'You did so, too!'

'Stop telling lies. Dad, giving him a hiding.'

'You did so swear.'

'I bloody well did not!'

'Ooooo! Dad! She swore again!'

Georgina wails. Dad doesn't like swearing.

'But Da-aad. Hema started first with his spying.'

Dad gives a sigh.

'Lord preserve me. Quit it, you two! Have pity on your suffering father.'

'Yes, quit it!' Mum also growls. 'No time for quarrelling today, we're running late as it is. Hema! What took you so long? Did you have to make that milk!'

'It was Gina's fault, Mum,' Hema says. 'She didn't set the fire for this morning and I had to go out and get the wood myself.'

'Oooo! You big liar. Let me get at him, just let me get at him!'

Mum grabs Georgina and thrusts her into a chair by the table.

'Oh no you don't, Gina,' she says. 'You just sit at the table and have your kai. And you too, son! Where's that Hine? Hine, stop trying to make yourself beautiful and come to the table!'

Hema sits at the table opposite Gina. She tries to kick him underneath the table and he mouths taunts at her without saying the words.

(Ha-ha, ha-ha, you-missed-me, you-missed-me.)

(Not that time I didn't), Georgina mouths back. She smiles with supreme delight at the sight of Hema's pain. He bares his teeth at her.

(I'll fix you, Ugly)

(Listen to who's calling who Ugly)

(You bee-eye-tee-see...)

'Hema!' Mum yells.

'Yes, Mum?' he answers. His mother is looking suspiciously at the milk in the can. Hmmmm.

'You been putting water into the milk again, haven't you!'

'Me?'

'Yes, you!' Mum says. She comes over to the table and rolls back her sleeve. 'Next time you put water in the milk, you'll feel my hand good and proper!'

'Yes, Mum,' Hema answers meekly. His mother turns her back and he pokes his tongue at her.

'You do that again, Hema,' Mum says, 'and you'll feel my hand right now!'

Hema gasps. How did she know?

'I've got eyes in the back of my head,' Mum informs him.

Hema shrivels, but Georgina is delighted.

'He's doing it again, Mum!' she says.

'Oooo, you liar!'

But Mum doesn't hear.

'Put your kai where your words come from!' she snaps.

The children settle to having their breakfast. Hema says:

'Pass me the butter, Gina.'

'Pass me the butter Gina what?' she taunts.

'Pass me the butter Gina please!'

But Gina just stares at him and doesn't bother.

'Mum!' Hema yells. 'Gina won't pass me the butter.'

'He never asked for it,' Gina answers.

'I did so!'

'No you didn't. Mum! Hema's reaching across the table!'

As quick as a flash, Mum is back and she slaps Hema's fingers with the flat of a knife. Ow!

'Now ask for the butter!' Mum says. 'We've got manners in this house! And you better remember it, boy.'

Hema scowls.

(Well?) Georgina mouths.

'May I please have the butter, sister dear?' he says sarcastically.

And Georgina gives a huge triumphant smile.

'Of course, brother dear!'

She passes the butter and he slaps it onto a piece of bread, still with his eyes peering furiously at his sister.

(I'll fix you!)

(Oh, yeah?)

(Just you wait, Tutae-face)

(Blacky)

(Piss-pot)

(Stink-bum)

Hema picks up the bread. He eyes it and his sister dangerously, pretends that the bread is her, and bites her head off.

'Have I got heathens for children?!' Dad roars. He has come from the bedroom and is tucking in his pants. 'In this house, we say grace first. And we all sit down together for our kai!'

'Yes, Dad,' Hema mutters.

'Mum! Hine! Come and sit down. Right! Now I'll say grace.'

The family bow their heads. Dad begins.

'For what we are about to receive and-Hema-if-you-   touch-that-piece-of-bread-I'll-crack-   you-over-the-head may the Lord make us truly grateful Amen.' 'Amen,' the family intone.

'So what's everybody waiting for?' Dad enquires. 'Hoe in!'

And breakfast proceeds. No more mouthings, no more bickering, because Dad is at the table. But as he is eating his porridge, Hema's mind is racing. Shall I ask him now? Go on, don't be afraid! But what if he says no? There's no harm in asking! I'm scared. The showdown has to come sooner or later! Okay, I will ask him! And so Hema puts his spoon down and gives three very obvious coughs.

'Have you got a cold, Son?' Dad asks.

'No.'

'Are you sick or something?'

'No.'

'Well then, eat up! This is good kai and I won't have it going to waste. Lord preserve me.' And he continues eating.

Hema picks up his spoon. But then he suddenly decides that it's now or never.

'Dad, I'd like-a-pair- of-long-pants,' he says in a rush. In the following silence, he takes a spoonful of porridge.

'Pardon?' Dad asks.

'A pair of pants, Dad.'

'What do you want a pair of pants for!' Mum enquires. But Dad interrupts.

'No, let the boy speak,' he says to Mum. 'He must have a reason for asking. Well, Hema?'

But before Hema can speak, Georgina butts in.

'Maybe he's getting cold knees,' she giggles.

'That'll be enough from you, girl!' Dad commands. 'Speak up, Hema!'

'Aw, Dad. All the other boys at school have got long pants and I'm the only one who hasn't. And I'm thirteen now.'

'That's no reason, son!' Dad says. 'Being the same as the rest of the crowd, that's no reason at all. You have to be worthy yourself of having long pants. You have to show you're capable of wearing them, and wearing them well.'

'Dad, I am,' Hema pleads. 'I'm a man now. I'm thirteen years old. Can't you see?'

'A man!' Georgina guffaws. 'How do you know, Hema? Have you got a girl into trouble?'

Dad gives her a steely glance.

'Is that supposed to be funny, Georgina? That'll be enough from you.'

Dad looks across at Hema. He sees his boy, embarrassed and pleading. And all of a sudden, he remembers what happened to him about this time. The memory is a shock and a revelation. It seems only yesterday that he was a boy; and now, here he is, a father, and Hema seems exactly like he was when he had first asked his own father for long pants.

'Yes, I suppose you are a man,' Dad thinks aloud. He looks at Mum. 'We'd better have a talk about this, eh, Mum?'

'Not with all these Big Ears flapping around the place,' she answers.

'Korero Maori?' Dad asks her. She nods her head. And they begin talking on the subject in the Maori tongue. Hema looks at Georgina.

(What are they saying?)

(I dunno. But you won't get your long pants.)

(Wanna bet?)

(You're still a kid, you little bee-you-gee-gee...)

And then Dad interrupts.

'Okay, Son, you can have your pair of long pants.'

And Hema's heart leaps and pirouettes with joy.

'When, Dad, when!'

'On Friday, when we go into town.'

'Oh, thank you, Dad.'

And then Georgina pipes up. She cries to Mum.

'Mum, it isn't fair! If Hema can have a pair of long pants, then I should be allowed to have a long dress. I'm older than he is.'

'Me too!' says Hine. 'Share and share alike!'

And Mum groans.

'See, Dad? I told you this would happen! Anyway Georgina, what's wrong with the long dress you already got!'

'It's out of date!' Georgina wails.

Dad sighs.

'Lord preserve me, I've got a daughter who follows the fashions now.' And he brushes Georgina's pleas away. Then he eyes his son. 'So you think you're a man now, son? Okay, then from today, you begin proving it.'

'Yes, Dad.'

'From now on, I expect you to not only put in your work at home but also help out in the community. Being a man means being responsible not only for yourself and your family but also for your iwi. Nani Tama told me the septic tank is blocked down at the marae so, this afternoon, after school, you can help me to fix it. Speaking of Nani Tama, he needs somebody clever to help him rewrite the whakapapa that was lost when his and Miro's house burnt down and to help him with our Treaty claim. You can go over to see him this evening and offer to do it. Who knows? You might learn more about being a man, and the obligations you have as a Maori, by doing that.'

'All that as well as his usual work?' Mum asks. 'Don't you think it's a bit much, Dad?'

Dad shakes his head.

'No, Mum. Hema is a man now and he understands, don't you son!'

'Yes, Dad,' Hema sighs dismally.

'And from now on, we don't just give pocket money; you earn it!'

'He's got to do the dishes too!' Georgina spits.

'No, men don't do dishes,' Dad says. 'It's about time Hine started doing some work around here.'

'Oh, Da-aad!' Hine wails.

But Dad puts his hands up to stop the commotion.

'I have spoken. So be it and all of you, get to it!'

The family sweeps into action. Georgina begins to clear the table. She glares murderously at Hema.

(You rat!)

(Ha-ha, ha-ha, Geor-giiinaa)

(I'll get you for this)

Hema gets up. He goes into his bedroom and gets dressed for school.

He may only be five foot two and a quarter inches tall, but he's a man now. Dad has said so. And then he hears Dad at the door. Dad has a sad look on his face.

'Don't be in too much of a hurry to be a man, Hema,' he whispers. 'When you're a boy you can stay at the back. But when you're a man you have to go to the front.'

Then he is gone.

Humming to himself, Hema checks his appearance and then goes to feed the dogs. And suddenly, he remembers all the chores he has to do this morning. And the new jobs that Dad has begun piling on him.

And as he goes down the steps of the back verandah, the vision of being a man becomes suddenly appalling.

Hema swears to himself. He is thirteen years old and now he has to do more work! What an awful thought! He already does enough around this blankety blank place. When he was a kid, life was free and easy. Now that he's a man, he's got more responsibility.

He wanders down the path and past the henhouse. The hens cackle and gloat about him.

'Shut up, you bloody fowls!' Hema rages. And his breath explodes upon the morning air.

Why is he thirteen? Who wants to be more than five feet two and a quarter inches tall! Everybody picks on him. They make him a man before he's ready. The whole world is against him.

It just isn't fair.

ONE SUMMER MORNING

You can't imagine what it was like to be writing in London through 1971, stuck in that bed-sitting room with the city shouting 'Come out! Come out! Come and play!' But I wasn't writing all the time; I liked to play truant with the many friends Jane and I had made in the city and ... well ... I was lucky that I had discovered through my training in writing radio stories how to write fast, in the moment, and without thinking of what I was doing – the words just came up and out of me without hitting the sides. I think that having one leg still in one culture but the other leg now stretching to stand in London also helped to increase the emotion going into the stories; that further distance, I suspect, increased their sense of nostalgia.

Partway through our holiday, Jane and I made a mad dash to Paris, and we also bought a minivan and made trips around the countryside, coaxing the minivan through Wales to the Highlands of Scotland and back, sleeping in it on the way. I had a small notebook with me and was making notes for stories – writing *through* life rather than waiting for writing time to come along – and typing them up when we returned to London. By the time 1971 ended I had completed the stories and the novel, *Tangi,* packaged them up and sent them by airmail back to New Zealand.

'One Summer Morning' was in that package. It deals with the time when, after living for some years at Haig Street, Dad bought a farm on the Whakarau road, Te Karaka. Although we still kept the house in town at Haig Street, Mum and Dad shifted us out there when I was thirteen. By that time my sisters and I had been joined by my brother Derek. Two more siblings, Neil and Gay, were still to come, ten years later – making us eight all told, including a brother, Thomas, who died as an infant.

Although the work was hard, I loved living on the farm. Sure it was isolated, no electricity, no flushing toilet, but I had my sisters and brothers to play with and, in particular, a loving father and mother. I was also discovering, in the writing process, the 'character' – young, Maori, male, unafraid and with a huge moral compass – that I was to use later in my novels, such as *Bulibasha, King of the Gypsies.* Most of my young Maori male narrators, like Hema in 'One Summer Morning' or Tawhai in 'The Makutu on Mrs Jones', are adolescent, on the edge of adulthood, and about to make a discovery either about themselves or about the world they are walking towards. In a lot of cases that involves a sense of loss, but there is also a sense of expectation that they will meet the challenges that will face them. They reach their apotheosis in Simeon, the rebellious son in *Bulibasha, King of the Gypsies.* So, too, do the parents and siblings in 'One Summer Morning', who become Joshua and Huria and the daughters Faith, Hope and Glory in the novel.

I like to think that when *Pounamu Pounamu* did achieve success as a school text, 'One Summer Morning' put out a message that, hey, puberty was exciting and something to look forward to. In those days, New Zealand fiction didn't find much in puberty to laugh about. However, it is also because of 'One Summer Morning' that *Pounamu Pounamu* was banned in one school district in the South Island.

My sister, Caroline, still lives on the farm today.

THE CHILD

'Haere mai, mokopuna,' she would say.

And always I would go with her, for I was both her keeper and her companion. I was a small boy; she was a child too, in an old woman's body.

'Where we going today, Nani?' I would ask. But I always knew.

'We go down to the sea, mokopuna, to the sea.'

Some people called my Nani crazy, porangi. Whenever I heard that word, my heart would flutter as if a small bird was trapped in there and wanted to get out. My Nani wasn't porangi, not to me.

But always, somebody would laugh at her and play with her feeble mind as if it was a kaitaka, a top which you whipped with flax to keep spinning. They would mimic her too, the sudden spasms that shook her body or the way she used to rock her head when her mind was wandering far away.

Dad, he told me that those people didn't understand or that they were only joking. But I'd see the sharp flints gleaming in their eyes and the cruel ways they lashed out at her. I would yell, 'Stop! Don't you make fun of my Nani.' I used to hate them all.

I loved my Nani. I would pat her on the head and hug her close to me. And she would whimper and put her arms around me too.

'Where my kete,' she would ask me. 'Where my kete?'

And I would help her look for it. I knew always that the basket would be under her bed, but Nani liked playing pretend so I'd play along with her.

'I don't know, Nani,' I'd tell her as we searched in all the dark corners of her room. 'Is it in the drawer? No, not there. In the wardrobe? No. Might be in the corner, eh? No. Where you put it, Nani? Where?'

And all the time, she would answer me in a vague voice, just like a little girl.

'I don' know, mokopuna. I don' know where I put my kete. It's somewhere. Somewhere here, somewhere.'

We'd play the game a little longer. Then I'd laugh.

'Here it is, Nani! Here's your bag!'

Her eyes would light up.

'You found it, mokopuna? You found my kete? Ae, that's it, that my kete.'

I would put it in her hands.

'You ready to go now, Nani?' I'd ask. 'We go down to the sea now?'

'I put my scarf on first, eh,' she would answer. 'Might be cold, might be makariri.'

Those other people, they never saw my Nani the way I did. And some of the kids at school they used to be funny to her. Willie Anderson, he would make faces and act all crazy. He would follow Nani and imitate the way she walked. His father caught him once, and gave him a good hiding. But Willie didn't feel sorry; he only hated Nani more. And he told lies about her. We had a fight after school one day. He was tougher than me and he won. But I didn't care, not even when he told some other kids I was porangi too.

I had my Nani; I didn't need anybody else.

'You fellas just leave my Nani alone,' I told them. 'Don't you touch her even.'

Willie, he just laughed and threw dust at me.

But he was only jealous, because he'd thought that when Nani was staring in the sky, she was looking at nothing.

'No! I've seen what she looks at, Willie Anderson, I've seen her world. She's taken me there.'

Willie didn't like that. He never liked being left out of things. That's why he was jealous.

'Come to me, Nani,' I would say.

And she would come and lift her head so that I could put her scarf on her. She would sit very still and very silent, and her lips would move without saying anything. The words were soundless.

'Yes, Nani,' I would answer. 'We're going down to the sea soon. Just wait your hurry. No don't say bad words to me. Nani! I heard what you said that time! You're a bad girl!'

My Nani, she knew when I was angry with her. Her eyes would dim and she would fold her hands carefully in her lap. Sometimes, a small drop of spittle would trickle from her mouth.

'I'm sorry, mokopuna,' she would whisper slowly.

I'd wipe her lips.

'Don't cry, Nani. I was only playing. Don't be a crybaby, don't be a tangiweto!'

And her eyes would light up, and deep down in them I'd see a little girl beginning to smile.

'You're cunning all right, Nani!' I would say. 'Those are only pretending tears! I know you, Nani! So no more cry, eh? Come on, we go to the sea now. Haere mai.'

And she'd put her hand in mine.

My Nani, she used to be all right once. She never used to be porangi all the time. And she had another life, another history, way before I was born.

'Your Nani was with Te Kooti the prophet when he took the people to Ohiwa,' Dad told me. 'She's one of the morehu, the Ringatu survivors, of the Pakeha wars. During the 1918 flu epidemic she took all the children into the bush and didn't bring us out until it was over. If it wasn't for her we wouldn't be here today. Over all these years she has protected and nurtured the seed sown at Raiatea.'

'Where you going, Tawhai?' Mum would ask.

And I would tell her, sometimes afraid that she might say, 'No, you and Nani stay home.'

'Me and Nani,' I would answer, 'we're going down to the beach for a little walk. Won't be long, Mum.'

'Okay, but you look after Nani, eh. If it gets cold, you put your jersey around her. If it starts to rain, you bring her home straight away. And don't get up to any mischief down there.'

'All right, Mum.'

And I would turn to my Nani.

'Come on, Nani. It's all right. Mum said we could go. Come on, come to me, Nani. Give me your hand. Don't be afraid.'

And together, we'd walk out of the house.

Sometimes, my Nani she'd be just like she used to be, as if she was waking up from a long moe. She'd laugh and talk and her body wouldn't shiver all the time. But after a while, her mind would go to sleep again.

When she was asleep like that, I'd have to help her do things. Nani couldn't even feed herself when her mind went away!

'Come to me, Nani,' I would say. And she'd sit down, and I'd put a tea towel around her neck to stop the kai from getting on her dress. 'Open your mouth, Nani. Wider yet. That's it. There we are! Wasn't that good? This kai's good eh!' And she'd nod her head and make her moaning noises which meant she wanted some more. So I'd fill her spoon again, and she would smile to show she was happy.

'What that thing?' Nani would ask as we walked along the road.

And she would point to a house, a tree, a car or an animal grazing in a paddock. She liked pretending she didn't know what things were.

'That's a horse, that's a fowl, that's where Mrs Katene lives, that's a kowhai,' I would tell her.

And she would repeat my words in a slow, sing-song voice.

'A tree, a manuka, a fence, a horse. No, that's not a horse, that's a hoiho, mokopuna.'

'That's right, Nani!' I would say. 'You're cleverer than me, eh! You know all the Maori names; I don't, Nani. Your mokopuna, he's dumb!'

And she would giggle and do a little dance. Sometimes, she'd even sing me a song.

Tahi nei taru kino
Mahi whaiaipo,
Kei te wehenga
Aroha kau ana.

And her quavering voice would lift its wings and circle softly in the air.

Nani liked to sing. Sometimes, she'd be waiting at the door for me when I got home from school, and she'd have the guitar in her hands. Kepa, my brother, he gave me that guitar and learned me a few chords. But I didn't know how to play it properly. Nani didn't mind, though. As long as I strummed it, she was happy. We'd sit on the verandah, she'd press my fingers to the strings, and as I played she would sing, one song after the other.

And sometimes, Dad would come and join us. 'What a racket!' he would say. 'Here, give that guitar to me.' And he would tune it and say to Nani, 'Come on, Mum, we sing your song, eh? Ready, steady, go!' My Dad, he could play that guitar! And him and Nani, they could sing as good as anything.

E puti puti koe, katoa hia
You're just a flower from an old bouquet,
I've waited patiently for you, each day

That was Nani's song. Her Pakeha name was Violet, and everybody called her that name because her Maori name was too long. And my Nani, she was just like a violet; shy and small and hiding her face in her petals if the sun blazed too strong.

'We're almost there now, eh, mokopuna,' Nani would say.

And I would nod my head.

'Ae, Nani. Almost there. Almost at the sea.'

Nani always said that same thing every time we reached the short cut to the beach. She'd hurry along the road to the gate. Beyond it, a path led through a paddock and down the cliff to where the sea was. Nani, she would run a little ahead of me, then look back just to make sure I was following. She didn't like being alone.

'Haere mai, mokopuna!' she would yell. 'Hurry up! The sea!'

And she would cock her head to the wind and hear the waves murmuring. Then she'd run along a little further and flutter her hands at me to hurry.

I used to pretend not to hear her, and just dawdle along.

'Eh, Nani? What you say?' I would call.

And always, she would flutter her hands and lean her head into the wind.

My Nani, she loved the sea. She and Nani Pita used to live in a house right on the beach. But when Nani Pita died, she came to live at our place because Dad was the eldest of her children. Dad, he told me that Nani wasn't really porangi; just old and lonely. He didn't know how long she'd stay with us because she was as old as Nani Pita.

'What is the greatest thing that we can do as a family, son?' he asked. 'It is to love and care for each other. Your Nani has loved us all her life, looked after us and fought many battles for us. It is only right that now she is old our turn has come to look after her. By loving her we honour her. By looking after her we truly begin to understand how painful as well as fulfilling love can be. Many people are not given this great gift of loving someone as old as she is. So while you have her, you love her, eh?'

I told him I would make Nani so happy that she would never want to leave. But Dad, he didn't understand that I knew my Nani wouldn't go away. He just smiled sadly and put his hands around my shoulders. 'Some day,' he said. 'Some day.'

Sometimes, late at night, I'd hear Nani crying because she was lonely. I'd creep softly down the corridor to her room and brush her tears away with my hands.

'You're too old to cry,' I'd growl her. But she'd keep weeping, so I'd hug her for a while. 'Turi turi, Nani,' I'd whisper. 'I'm here. Don't be afraid.'

And sometimes, I'd stay with her until she went to sleep again.

'Here's one, mokopuna!' she would yell. 'I got one!'

And she would hold up a sea shell she had found.

My Nani, she thought I liked shells; I don't know why. Maybe it was because when she first came to stay with us, she saw a paua shell in my room. Whatever it was, every time we went down to the sea, she'd wander along the beach, looking for shells to give to me.

'You want this one?' she'd ask. And she'd cock her head to one side and look into my eyes. Sometimes, she looked so hardcase that I'd laugh.

'Okay, Nani! We take it home.'

Then she'd look very happy and drop the shell into her kete.

'We taking you home,' she would tell the shell. 'We taking you home for my mokopuna.'

And every now and then, as we walked along the beach, she would let go of my hand to get another shell glittering on the sand.

'I already got enough, Nani!' I would yell.

But always, she would show it to me and cock her head as if she was asking a question.

'All right, Nani,' I would sigh. 'We take this one home too.'

It used to be good just wandering along the beach with Nani. If it was sunny and the sea wasn't rough, she'd let go of my hand more often, and wander off alone. I didn't mind, because I knew Nani wasn't really alone; she was wandering with Nani Pita on some remembered day.

But sometimes, a seagull would scream or cast its shadow over her head. Then she would stop and begin to tremble.

'It's all right, Nani,' I'd say. 'I'm here.'

And she would reach out for my hand.

'You won't leave me will you, mokopuna?' she would say.

'No, Nani,' I would answer. 'Turi turi now.'

And we would walk together again. Nani, she never left me when the sea was stormy. She used to be very scared and hold me very tight. Seaweed, it frightened her. She'd look at the waves and see the seaweed rising with them and whimper, afraid that she'd be caught by the long, black fingers.

And sometimes, she would make me scared too.

'We go back home now, eh?' I would ask her.

'Ae, we go home, mokopuna. Home.'

And she'd clutch her bag closely to her, and the shells would clink and scrape against each other.

One day, my Nani, she wasn't home when I got back from school. I looked in her room, I looked everywhere, but I couldn't find her. Mum got worried and went to get Dad. But I knew where she'd be.

I ran down the road.

'Nani! Nani!'

I don't know why I was crying. Perhaps it was because she had gone without waiting for me.

'Nani! Nani!'

I heard the sea murmuring as I ran along the path, toward the cliff. I looked down to the beach.

My Nani, she was lying there.

'Nani!'

I rushed down the cliff toward her. I hugged her to me.

In her hand was a sea shell.

'Yes, Nani,' I said. 'That's a good one, that's the best one you've ever found for me. We put it in your bag, eh? We take it home. We go home now, we go home...'

But she didn't answer.

Her mind had wandered far away, and my Nani, she had wandered after it.

'Haere mai, mokopuna,' she would say.

And always I would go with her.

'Where we going, Nani?'

'We go down to the sea, mokopuna. To the sea.'

THE CHILD

This story is about one of my other grandmothers, Nani Puti, whom my mother Julia brought home to stay with us because she was suffering from dementia. It was inspired by a memory of taking Nani for a walk along Wainui Beach.

'The Child', 'The Whale' and 'Tangi' are possibly the most elegiac of all the stories in *Pounamu Pounamu* and, in my opinion, certainly the richest, most poetic and best written. But around 2002, thirty years after the first publication of the collection, I realised that whereas the majority of stories in *Pounamu Pounamu* were waiata aroha, these three (plus 'Fire on Greenstone') were tonally different, more like waiata tangi. For instance, you could 'read' the four stories subtextually as conveying a world – Maori rural life and traditional culture – that was in decline or dying. 'The Child' was about the changing of generations, with the great influence of the kuia in decline because of the discontinuity of memory; the whale in the short story 'The Whale' was Maori culture itself, dying because the people were being influenced by Pakeha ways; and 'Tangi' was a story in which the traditional society, as personified in the father, is changing and the young son must find his own strength within a non-Maori world. But since 1972, Maori had sought sovereignty, tino rangatiratanga, and there were all the signs of a culture in transcendence.

This was why I rewrote *Pounamu Pounamu* in 2003. And so, for instance, the story 'Tangi' now ends subtly (I hope) with the addition of a traditional proverb: 'You are from a seed that was sown in Rangiatea and you will never be lost.'

I was like that seed, too, when Jane and I, after flying to Greece and taking a mad Tiki Tour bus trip around Europe, returned to New Zealand in early 1972. We arrived to the happy news that David Heap and Heinemann Educational had accepted *Pounamu Pounamu* and *Tangi* ... and a third book. This third book had originally been 'Village Sunday', a novella which I had written for inclusion as the final story of *Pounamu Pounamu*. David, along with

Maurice Dowthwaite, who was managing editor of Heinemann, considered that with an additional 25,000 words it could be published separately – which it was, with the title of *Whanau.*

THE WHALE

He sits, this old kaumatua, in the darkness of the meeting house. He has come to this place because it is the only thing remaining in his dying world.

In this whanau, this old one is the last of his generation. All his family, they have died: parents, brothers, sisters, relations of his generation, all gone. Ruia, his wife, she's been dead many years. His friends, there are none. Children, mokopuna, yes, there are many of those. But of his time, only he and this meeting house remain.

The meeting house...

This old one, he sighs, and the sound fills the darkness. He looks upon the carved panels, the tukutuku reed work, the swirling red and black and white kowhaiwhai designs, and he remembers he awoke to life here. That was long ago, another world ago, when this meeting house and whanau, this village, brimmed over with happiness and aroha. Always he has lived here. This meeting house has been his heart, his strength. He has never wished to leave it. In this place lie his family and memories. Some are happy, others are sad. Some are like dreams, so beautiful that they seem never to have existed. But his dreams died long ago. With each tangi, each funeral, they have died. And he is the last of the dreamers.

This kaumatua, his eyes dim. In this falling afternoon he has come to visit the meeting house for the last time. He knows it is the last time. Just as the sun falls and the shadows lengthen within the meeting house, so too is his life closing. Soon his photograph will be placed along the wall with those of his other friends, relations and tipuna—his ancestors.

This village has always been a proud place, ringing with joy. Its people are a proud people, a family. One great family, clustered around this meeting house. Ae, they quarrelled sometimes, but it is only the happiness that this old one remembers.

However, over the years, people have begun to leave in search of a new life. Many of the houses lie deserted. The fields are choked with weeds. The gorse creeps over the graveyard. And the sound of children laughing grows smaller each year.

That is the most heartbreaking thing of all. Once the manawa, the heart, throbbed with life and the whanau gave it life. But over the years more and more of its children left and the family began to break apart. Of those that went few returned. And the heartbeat is weaker now.

He sighs again, this kaumatua. He would like to stay but he has reached the end of his years. His people they will weep for him. Hera, his niece, she will cry very much. But in the end, she will remember.

'Hera, don't you be too sad when I'm gone. If you are, you come to this meeting house. I'll be here, Hera. You come and share your aroha with me. You talk to me; I will listen.'

He'd told her that when she was a little girl. Even then the world had been changing. Hera, she'd been one of the few of his mokopuna who'd been interested in the Maori of the past. The rest, they'd felt the pull of the Pakeha world, like fish too eager to grab at a dangling hook. In Hera he had seen the spark, the hope that she might retain her Maoritanga. And he had taught her all he knew.

'Hera, this is not only a meeting house; it is also the body of a tipuna, an ancestor. The head is at the top of the meeting house, above the entrance. That is called the koruru. His arms are the maihi, the boards sloping down from the koruru to form the roof. See the tahuhu, ridgepole? That long beam running from the front to the back along the roof? That is the backbone. The rafters, the heke, they are the ribs. And where we are standing, this is the heart of the house. Can you hear it beating?'

And Hera, she had listened and heard. She had clutched him, afraid.

'Koro! The meeting house, it lives!'

'The meeting house, it won't hurt you, Hera,' he had told her. 'You are one of its children. Turi turi now.'

And he had lifted the veils from the photographs of all her family dead and told her about them.

'That's your Nani Whiti. He was a brave man. This is my Auntie Hiria, she was very beautiful, eh? She's your auntie too. This man, he was a great rangatira.'

Later, they had sat in the middle of the meeting house, he on a chair, she sitting on the floor next to him, and he had told her its history.

'This meeting house, it is like a book, Hera. All the carvings, they are the pages telling the story of this whanau. The Pakeha, he says they're legends. But for me they are history.'

And page by page, panel by panel, he had recounted the history.

'That is Pou, coming from Hawaiki on the back of a giant bird. He brought the kumara to Aotearoa. This is Paikea, riding a whale across the sea to Aotearoa. He was told not to let the whale touch the land. But he was tired after the long journey, and he made the whale come to shore. It touched the sand, and became an island. You can still see it, near Whangara. See the tukutuku work on the walls? All those weavings, they represent the stars and the sky.'

And Hera, her eyes had glistened with excitement.

'Really, Koro, really?'

'Ae, Hera. You remember.'

This old one, he closes his eyes to keep the memories away because inevitably, as had happened with all the others, even Hera had gone away to the city. And when she had returned for a visit, this old one could see that she was finding it difficult to reconcile the Maori way with the Pakeha way. He had tried to lead her back to his world, and she had quarrelled with him.

'Don't, Koro! The world isn't Maori any more. But it's the world I have to live in. I know you want me to stay. But I can't.'

But he had been stubborn, this kaumatua. He'd always been stubborn. If she would not come back to his world, then she would take it to the city with her.

'Come, Hera, I want to show you something.'

'No, Koro.'

'These books, in them is your whakapapa, your ancestry. All these names, they are your family who lived long ago, traced back to the Horouta canoe. You take them with you when you go back.'

'Koro.'

'No, you take them. And see this space? You put my name there when I die. You do that for me. You keep this whakapapa safe. And don't you ever forget who you are. You're Maori, understand? You are Maori.'

His voice had been fierce and passionate, his words ringing with conviction. And Hera had embraced him and he felt her own strength.

'I understand Koro,' she had whispered. 'You taught me too well to be Maori. But you didn't teach me about the Pakeha world.'

He opens his eyes, this old one, but he still hears his Hera's whisper. Ae, he had taught her well. And one day her confusion would pass and she would find her way back. How? Through following the pathway of whakapapa and, through her journey, she would realise that belonging, being Maori, was truly what mattered. That's why he had taught her well. That's why.

For a moment he smiles to himself, this old one. Then he recalls an ancient saying. How old it is he does not know. Perhaps it had come with the Maori when he journeyed across the sea to Aotearoa. From Hawaiki. From Tawhiti-roa, Tawhitinui, Tawhiti-pamamao, the magical names for the first home of the Maori. No matter. Even before the Pakeha had come to this land, his coming had been foretold.

Kei muri i te awe kapara he tangata ke,
mana te ao, he ma.
Shadowed behind the tattooed face a stranger stands,
he who owns the earth, and he is white.

And with his coming, the tattooed face had changed. That was the way of things, relentless and unalterable. But the fighting spirit of the Maori, did that need to change as well? Ae, even in his own day, Maoritanga had been dying. But not the fighting spirit, not the joy or aroha.

He cannot help it, this kaumatua, but the anger rises within him.

The Maori language has almost gone from this whanau. The respect for Maori customs and Maori tapu, that too was disappearing. No more did people take their shoes off before coming into this meeting house. The floor is scuffed with shoemarks. The tukutuku work is pitted with cigarette burns. And even the gods and tipuna, they have been defaced. A name has been chipped into a carved panel. Another panel bears a deep scratch. And a paua eye has been prised from a carved figure, a wheku.

This meeting house, it had once been noble. Now, the red ochre is peeling from the carvings. The reed work is falling apart. The paint is flaking from the swirling kowhaiwhai designs. And the floor is stained with the pirau, the beer, for even that has been brought into this meeting house.

And the young, not understanding custom, do not come to this meeting house with respect, nor with aroha. They look with blind eyes at the carvings and do not see the beauty and strength of spirit which is etched in every whorl, every bold and sweeping spiral. They too are the strangers behind the tattooed face.

Is it their fault? this old one wonders. Is it their fault that so many families had to leave in search of work? That the younger generation grow up not knowing their papakainga? He has seen too many of his people come as strangers. The Maori of this time is different from the Maori of his own time. The whanau, the family, and the aroha which binds them together as one heart, is breaking, slowly loosening. The children of the whanau seek different ways to walk in this world. Before, there was a sharing of aroha with one another. No matter how far away some of the children went there was still the aroha which bound them closely to this meeting house and village. But the links are breaking. The young grow apart from each other. They walk away and do not come back. That is why the old one's heart beats so loud with anger. The language, the customs, the knowledge—matauranga Maori—must be brought back.

'Aue! Aue!'

This kaumatua, he fills the meeting house with the sound of his grief. After all, it was his task, surely, to transmit the knowledge to the new generation.

'Aue! Aue!'

And from his grief springs a memory which adds to his despair. Of a time not long ago, when people from all Aotearoa gathered at this meeting house to celebrate the wedding of a child of this whanau.

The visitors, they had come from the Taranaki, from the Waikato, from the many parts of Te Ika a Maui, even from Te Waipounamu—the South Island. They had arrived for the hui throughout the day. By car, by bus, by train they had come, and the manawa of this whanau had beaten with joy at their gathering together.

It had been like his own time, this old one remembers. The children laughing and playing around the meeting house. The men and women renewing their friendships. The laughing and the weeping. The sweet smell of the hangi, and the sudden clouds of steam as the kai was taken from the earth. The girls swaying past the young men, eyeing the ones they wanted. The boys standing together, both bold and shy, but hiding their shyness beneath their jokes and bantering. The kuias gossiping in the cookhouse. The big wedding kai, and the bride and groom pretending not to hear the jokes about their first night to be spent together. The singing of the old songs. The cooks coming into the hall in their gumboots and old clothes to sing with the guests:

Karangatia ra! Karangatia ra!
Powhiritia ra, nga iwi o te motu
Ki runga o Turanga. Haere mai!
Call them! Call them!
Welcome them, the people of the land
Coming onto this marae, Turanga.
Welcome!

Ae, it had indeed been like the old times. The laughter and the joy had sung through the afternoon into the night. And he had sat with the other old men, watching the young people dancing in the hall.

Then it had happened. Late in the night. Raised voices. The sound of quarrelling.

'Koro! Come quick!'

A mokopuna had grabbed his hand and pulled him outside, along the path to the dining room. More visitors had arrived. They had come from the Whangarei, and they were tired and hungry. He saw their faces in the light. But people of his whanau, they were quarrelling with the visitors. They would not open the door to the storeroom. It was locked now. There would be no kai for these visitors. They had come too late. Heart was locking out heart.

He had been stunned, this old one. Always there was food, always aroha, always open heart. That was the Maori way. Aroha.

And he had said to his mokopuna:

'Te toki. Homai te toki. The axe. Bring me the axe.'

The crowd had heard his whispered fury. They parted for him. His tokotoko, his walking stick, it supported him as he approached the door. The music stopped in the hall. The kanikani, the dancing, stopped. People gathered. His fury gathered. The axe in his hand. He lifted it and...

'Aue.'

The first blow upon the locked door.

'Aue.'

His anger showing in his face.

'Aue.'

The wood splintering beneath the blade.

'Aue.'

His heart splintering too.

He gave his anger to the axe. He gave his sorrow to the blows upon the door. The axe rose and fell, rose and fell, and it flashed silver from the light.

Then it was done. The door gave way. Silence fell. He turned to the visitors. His voice was strained with agony.

'Haere mai, e te manuhiri. Haere mai. Haere mai. Come, visitors. Come. Enter.'

He had opened his arms to them. Then, trembling, he had pointed at the splintered door.

'Anei ra toku whakama ... See? Look upon my shame.'

Then he had walked away, not looking back. Away from the light into the darkness.

This kaumatua, the memory falls away from him. He sees the darkness gathering quickly in the meeting house.

How long has he been here, contemplating the changing world?

This old one, he grips his tokotoko and stands. Aue, he has lingered too long. One last look at this meeting house. The carved panels glint in the darkness. The kowhaiwhai designs flash with the falling sun. The evening wind flutters the black veils which hang upon the photographs of his dead.

So still he stands, this kaumatua, that he seems to merge into the meeting house and become a carved figure himself. Then his lips move. One last whisper to this meeting house, and he turns and walks away.

'No wai te he?'

He walks along the dusty road, through the village. The houses are clustered close together. A truck speeds past him.

'No wai te he?'

He hears a gramophone blaring loudly from one of the houses. He sees into a lighted window, where the walls are covered with glossy pictures that have been carefully cut out of magazines. A group of young people are gathered around another house, laughing and singing party songs. They beckon him to come and join them.

'No wai te he?'

Down the path from the village he goes, to where his own house lies on the beach, apart from the village. Through the manuka, down the cliff to the sand he walks. The sea is calm, the waves softly rippling. And far away the sun is setting, slowly drowning in the water.

'No wai te he?'

Then he sees a cloud of gulls blackening the sky. Their guttural screams fill the air. They dive and swoop and cluster upon a dark mound, moving feebly in the eddying water.

And as the old one approaches, he sees that it is a whale, stranded in the breakwater, threshing in the sand, already stripped of flesh by the falling gulls. The water is washed with red, the foam flecked with blood.

He cries out then, this kaumatua, raging against the gulls.

'No wai te he ... Where lies the blame ... the blame.'

Where lies the blame, the blame.....

The gulls shriek and wheel away from him. And in their claws they clasp his shouted words, battling and circling against one another with a flurry of black wings.

THE WHALE

I was twenty-eight when *Pounamu Pounamu* was published in 1972. When I look at the photograph of myself on the back of the hardcover jacket I can scarcely recognise myself. The blurb invited readers to look through the greenstone ... Memory is that David and Maurice wanted to give the book the best shot at success they could because, now, instead of it being a book solely for the educational market, they saw possibilities of it crossing over into the general, mainly Pakeha, market. To use the metaphor of a game of cards again, they wanted to make sure we had a good hand – and frankly, I needed all the help I could get.

I doubt whether any young author could have had a better publisher than David, who became a trusted friend. He and Maurice had great success with the *Auckland Star* (I suspect Harry Dansey, who was working as Maori reporter at the time, had something to do with it), which ran one story from the collection every Saturday for six weeks. They also decided to send me on a book tour, signing copies and speaking to the local Rotary and other groups in small towns throughout the country. My minder was Ted Bland, a terrifically buoyant guy, which was just as well because I was like an opossum transfixed by the lights of a truck. The local media turned up and the speaking events were well attended, except for one town hall appearance in Greytown. There, an old kuia and her grandson were the only members of the audience. She said to me, 'The moko wanted to come.'

Well, all I could think of was all my grandmothers and how they had nurtured me; and, although it was suggested we cancel, I remembered the saying, 'Where you see one, you see a thousand.' So I spoke to my audience of two about my life, and I told the boy how important his grandmother was; he seemed to know that already.

Afterwards, the old lady insisted that I go and stay with her at their place. Lucky Ted Bland got to go back to his nice hotel, while I got taken to this whare in the bush somewhere, where I made the mistake – not realising the kuia was not on town supply – of asking if I could take a bath. So she heated some water in a copper, and she and her moko filled the bath bucket by bucket, and then I had to take my clothes off under the moon and suffer her ministrations and scolding as she soaped me up and washed me.

How did I feel? Like a puppy dog, in absolute bliss.

Although there's not much bliss in 'The Whale', what's important about this story can be said about the whole collection: *Pounamu Pounamu* provided a 'greenprint' for all my fiction to come. The same characters in all these stories turn up throughout my fiction. The tribal clans of Waituhi appear in *The Matriarch, Whanau* and *Whanau II, The Dream Swimmer* and *Bulibasha, King of the Gypsies,* and so on. And the family in 'One Summer Morning', although not named, becomes the Mahana family in my fiction, the Maori equivalent of Katherine Mansfield's Burnell family.

As far as 'The Whale' is concerned, I was able to rework the elements in my novel, *The Whale Rider,* and turn its themes into something redemptive and triumphant.

TANGI

One step further now.

Do not listen to the wailing, Tama. Do not listen to the women chanting their sorrows, the soaring waiata tangi which sings alone and disconsolate above the wailing. It is only the wind, Tama. Do not listen to the sorrow of the marae.

Do not look up, Tama. The marae is strung with electric bulbs and black shadows walk within the blazing light. If you look up, you will see the many faces of grief, every face pale and shrouded in the dark garments of mourning. You will see your father where he lies on the cold stone and your mother keeping vigil over him this long night. Do not look up. Else you will be lost.

'Mr Mahana? Gisborne calling, Mrs Kingi on the line.'

'Hello, Marama!'

'Hello, Tama.'

My sister's voice is calm and soft. She pauses for a moment.

'You'll have to come home, Tama. Dad's dead.'

Daddy, why did my Nani Teria die?

Because she was old.

Are you old, Daddy?

No, Tama.

Don't grow old, Daddy. Please, don't grow old.

Step firmly, Tama. One step. Now the next. Although the earth may sway and reel under your feet, step firmly. The earth sorrows with you.

Step firmly, Tama.

'How's Mum, Marama?'

'She's taking it well, Tama. She helped wash Dad's body, got him ready, dressed him ... he was so heavy. We took him to Rongopai this morning.'

Daddy, why did we bring our Nani here?

Because Rongopai is our meeting house, Tama. This was where she was born, where I was born, where you were born. This is our home, Tama. And on the hill next to the meeting house is where all our people are buried. I will be buried there one day.

No you won't, Daddy.

One day, Son.

The shadow of an old man advances across the light. It is your grand-uncle, Tama. He is welcoming you home to the funeral of your father. Listen to his words, listen. But do not look up. The old man is chanting your whakapapa, your lineage, and your links with Rongopai. His voice threads itself within the sad wailing. Listen to the words, Tama. But do not look up. Not yet. Wait until his welcome is ended and the silence falls within which every ear strains to hear your reply. Not yet, Tama.

'Quite suddenly, about three o'clock this morning. Mum woke up and there he was, cold, lying beside her. Mum rang me about five, you know how early Mum gets up. So me and Hata went out to her, and you know what Mum was doing? There she was, sitting beside Dad, just knitting, knitting a jersey for Dad, waiting for us, knitting, just knitting.'

'Oh, Marama.'

When the welcome is ended, Tama, then you may look up. Look your grand-uncle proudly in the face and do not think of tears. The wailing will sigh away like a drifting wind. Then will be the time to speak.

'Anything wrong, Tama?'

Mr Ralston puts his hands on my shoulders. I turn. He sees my tears.

'My father, my father is dead, Mr Ralston. I must go home, Mr Ralston, pack my bags and go home. My father is dead.'

Daddy, why does the man throw Nani Teria's suitcases and photographs and things in the hole?

Because that is where Nani is, Tama. And because that is our way. What do we need Nani's things for?

Has my Nani really gone now?

Yes, Son. She's gone now and you've got no Nani any more.

She was a good Nani, wasn't she Daddy. Why did she have to go into the earth?

Do not think of sorrow, Tama. You must make your father proud. Send your words loud and ringing that he may hear. Bear yourself with pride. Answer your grand-uncle's loving words with your own. Address the assembly, Tama.

'Was your father an old man?'

'No, Mr Ralston. About fifty-seven.'

I watch the windscreen wipers swish across the window, sweeping away the rain.

'He was a good man, Mr Ralston.'

The telephone poles bend past. And here is Wellington Airport, glistening and wet.

It always rains when a Maori dies, Tama.

Why, Daddy?

The wailing makes the sky sad, and even if it is a bright summer day and there are no clouds, it rains. The sky mourns for your Nani too, Tama. She was a good woman.

Now is the time to speak, Tama. Proclaim to all who stand on the marae that you are Tama Mahana, eldest son of Rongo Mahana who was the son of Eruera Mahana. That you are of the Whanau A Kai, that your lineage is long and renowned. Proclaim that Rongopai is your family hearth, your birthright, and that you are pleased to stand before your whare tupuna. Let all who hear you know that you are indeed a Mahana. It is a proud name and your people are a proud people. You must be proud, Tama.

'I'm afraid, Marama.'

The lights of Waituhi are near and already I can hear the sorrows of Rongopai marae whispering in the wind.

'Almost there, Tama.'

The car turns into the gateway, the headlights flickering across the marae.

'I'm afraid, Marama.'

'Kia kaha, Tama. Be strong.'

I close my eyes, tightly, tightly closed.

Where are you, Daddy?

I'm here, Son.

I cannot feel your hand, Daddy. Hold my hand so that I know that you are here with me. It is dark and I am afraid. Hold my hand.

One step. Then one step further now.

After you have completed the initial ceremonials, Tama, let your voice be small so that every person among the assembly must strain to hear your words. Tell them that grief is in your heart and your body is a dark and empty shell in which your thoughts gather and produce tears. Tell them that you have come home to do homage to your father.

Hush, Tama. Do not cry so much.

But she was a good Nani, she was good to me, Daddy.

Then it is right for you to weep, Tama. But never forget that the sun always rises.

When, Daddy? When?

Do not falter, Tama. Remember that you are your father's son. You are the eldest son and the example is yours to set. Do not let your voice drift, as if it were an empty canoe adrift on the sea. Take up the paddle, strike deep into the water. Look upon your mother where she sits weeping. She is your guiding star. Point your prow toward that star and let her know that you are here.

'Let me speak to Mum, Marama.'

I hear my mother weeping softly, softly, and I cannot restrain my sorrow. For she is my mother and I am her son.

'Hello, Tama.'

'Mum, are you all right? Mum, don't cry Mum.'

'Come home,' my mother says. 'Come home, come home, come home, come home.'

Over and over again, she calls to me.

'Mum, please don't cry Mum, please.'

'Come home, Son, come home and comfort me. I am alone now. Come home, come home.'

You must always look after your younger sisters and brothers, Tama. Your mother too, if I should die. Remember, Tama, always.

Yes, Daddy.

You are the eldest. That is your duty, your obligation. I was taught that as a child. I teach you that now.

Be at peace, Tama. You spoke well and you were your father's son. Be at peace. But do not rest. Look upon the mourners. They come from the shadows and from the light to share their grief with you. Haere mai, mokopuna, the old people whisper. Come and press noses with us and let us join our sorrow. Haere mai, mokopuna. Do not be too sad for we also grieve with you.

'We're truly sorry, Tama.'

'Thanks Mr Ralston. Thanks Tim. Thanks Bob.'

I must shake the hands of my friends and receive their condolences. Yet if I look into their faces they look away from me, as if death is something that should not be admitted.

'We're truly sorry, Tama.'

Why are they sorry, Daddy? Why are they sad?

Because your Nani Teria was a good lady. Some of them realise now. And now they are sad.

Is that why they kiss her? Must I kiss her?

You won't see your Nani after this day.

Then one last kiss, Nani.

I bend down upon my Nani's body. Nani does not breathe any more.

Goodbye, Nani.

Your people mourn with you, Tama. Embrace them and let them weep on your shoulder. The men weep, the women weep, the children weep because the men and women weep. This is a sad day. These are the people of your whanau. You have lost a father. They also have lost a father, a brother, a son, a friend. This is your family, this is your home. You are their son too, Tama.

'Auntie Mina came from Tauranga this morning,' Marama says. 'And Uncle Pita arrived this afternoon. Uncle Pita's been a great help. He did all the arrangements at Rongopai. Jackie and Arapata dug the hangi. A lot of people are coming. A lot of people to feed. Don't know where we're going to put them all.'

'What about in the old homestead, at Nani's place?'

'Yes, some there. But most of them in a marquee near the meeting house. The homestead is too small.'

Don't close the door, Daddy. Leave it open so that there is light. As long as I see the light burning, I'm not afraid.

You shouldn't be afraid, Tama. You're a big boy now.

And it is time to get on with life. The sun always rises. You are a seed that was sown at Raiatea.

One step. Then one step further now, to where my father lies alone and lonely under the harsh light.

Listen, Tama. A lone voice sings among the soft sounds of mourning. The voice of a kuia, your Auntie Ruihi. She sings an ancient lament which soars and swoops and curls above the hushed assembly. Look where she comes, slowly stepping from the darkness, her black gown threaded with green leaves, her hands outstretched, in each hand a sprig of greenery. She performs movements to her song. Slowly her hands move, with intricate precision, telling of the grief which tears at her heart. Some of the mourners join her song and perform the movements along with her. But she looks straight ahead, her face luminous with grief. She looks at you, Tama, her brother's son. Only you.

I watch my Nani going away into the earth. The earth is soft and wet because it is raining. Daddy's hands are tight upon my shoulders.

Nani's belongings are thrown into the hole. I see a picture of Nani fall. The glass smashes, but she is still smiling.

Goodbye, Nani.

Dirt falls upon Nani, shovel after shovel. And as she disappears, Auntie Ruihi starts a frenzied wailing.

Auntie Ruihi, please don't cry. Please Auntie, don't cry, don't, please.

Listen to your aunt's lament, Tama. Listen. She opens her arms to you. Through the spray of my gushing tears, she sings, I see you, my brother's son. Come weep with me, our anchor is gone, and we are cast adrift at the mercy of the sea.

Embrace your aunt, Tama. Weep with her. You have only lost a father. She has lost both parents and now her eldest brother. She has nobody who will look after her now. Weep with her, Tama. Kiss her once more. Aue, mokopuna, she weeps. Aue, aue, as she dissolves into the darkness.

You are alone now. Your father is on the marae. Your mother and brothers and sisters wait for you to join them by their father's side.

One step. Then one step further now.

You must always look after your brothers and sisters. And your mother too, if I should die.

'Are you all right, Mum?'

'Come home, Tama. Come home, come home, come home.'

'Mum just sits beside Dad, knitting, knitting a jersey for him, knitting, just knitting.'

'Come home, Son. Come home, come home.'

Step firmly, Tama. Do not listen to the wailing. It is only the wind shifting, only the wind renewing. Be proud. Your father waits among the flower wreaths. His body is draped with feather cloaks. Be proud.

'You'll have to come home, Tama. Dad's dead.'

We won't need Nani's things. That is why they are buried with her.

'I'm afraid, Marama.'

'Kia kaha, Tama. Be strong.'

Almost there, Tama. Almost there. The long journey almost at an end. See? Your brothers and sisters raise their arms to greet you. One step. Now another. And one step further now.

Are you old, Daddy, like my Nani Teria is old?

No, Tama.

Don't grow old, Daddy.

One day I will be old. Then I shall die.

No you won't. I won't let you.

One day, Tama.

Embrace your brothers and sisters, Tama, and be strong. You are the eldest. Embrace your mother, Tama. Do not listen to the wailing. Now, slowly look upon your father. Rest your arms on his casket and weep for him.

Daddy, where are you? It is dark and I can hear the wailing coming from the marae.

He was an old man, Tama. See how he sleeps. His eyes are closed and his face is pale in the blazing light. He is covered with feather cloaks. His face is cold. His hands are cold. The wind blows upon him and ruffles his grey hair. For three days he will lie here. Then on the afternoon of the third day, his casket will be closed and you will not see him again. On that day, you will help carry him up the hill to the family graveyard. He will be heavy, but you must be strong. It will rain. It always rains when a Maori dies. Then he will be covered by the earth.

This is the last goodbye, Tama.

Bend towards him, Tama.
One last kiss, Father. Your lips, so
cold, so cold.
Goodbye, Father.

Daddy, is it always so dark?
No, son, the sun always rises.
Always.
Soon, Daddy?
Soon. And never forget, Tama:

E kore au e ngaro
He kakano i ruiruia mai
i Rangiatea

You are from a seed that was
sown
in Rangiatea and you
will never be lost.

TANGI

This story had so many incarnations. I first wrote it way back in 1970 in Barry Mitcalfe's class, where it was called 'The Faraway Side of the Hour'. It was renamed 'Tangi' by Margaret Orbell and Tim Curnow when they read it in *Exercises for the Left Hand* and published it in *Contemporary Maori Writing* (1972), the first anthology of contemporary creative writing by Maori writers ever. I wrestled with the form of this story, not realising that the counterpointed nature of the narrative between the boy's thoughts on death, the tangi of his father and the embedded story of the events leading up to the funeral was supplying me with a poetic structure for a longer work. I began that longer work after talking on the phone from London with my mother.

'Hello, Mum? I'm thinking about writing a novel, but it's about a boy who goes back to Waituhi for the tangi of his father.'

'You're *what!* But Dad's still alive.'

'I know that, but this will be fiction.'

'I don't care what you call it, people at Waituhi will think it's about Tom. Oh well, you better write it before Dad dies, and then people will know it's just your usual make-believe.'

You'll never know the agony I went through while writing the novel. Of course I knew Dad wouldn't die while I was writing it, but you never could tell ... if he did, I realised that I would have to tell David the novel must be scrapped.

Well, Dad lived to a wonderful old age, he became my longest and best friend, and *Pounamu Pounamu* was followed by *Tangi* in 1973 and then *Whanau* in 1974.

But that was all in the future.

As for *Pounamu Pounamu* itself, it is the spring at the beginning of my writing career. One of the greatest thrills was when it was published in a Maori language version with a translation by Jean Wikiriwhi, becoming the first book of fiction in New Zealand to be translated and published in Maori.

The water from *Pounamu Pounamu* is still as clear, sparkling, fresh; and it reminds me that I have always in my life been greatly loved. Even today, when I am trying to find my way back to Maori stories, I always like to come back to that spring and drink of its clear water and try to share that love, that aroha, with others.

Seek always to attain
excellence, equity and justice.
If you must bow your head let it be
only to the highest mountain

Tena koutou katoa.

Witi Ihimaera

www.ingramcontent.com/pod-product-compliance
Lightning Source LLC
Chambersburg PA
CBHW071201100726
47908CB00002B/468